ELLIPSES II...

PSYCH WARD

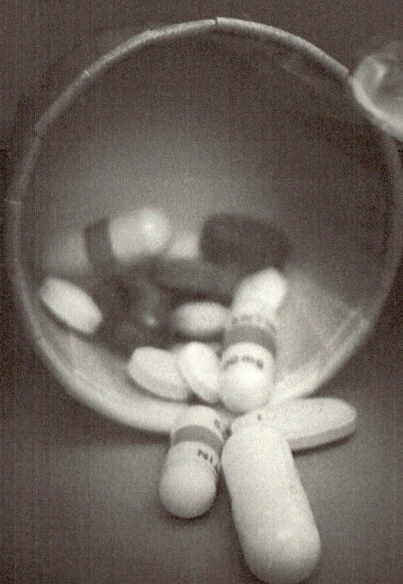

DEZI GOLDEN

ELLIPSES II...

DEZI GOLDEN

First printing: December 2023

Ebook ISBN: 979-8-9898431-0-7
Paperback ISBN: 979-8-9898431-1-4

Visit www.dezigolden.com for autographed copies.

To those who believe in change...but the heart remaining...

This is for you...
and for P-

Chapter 1

PEG

Peg turned down the street and slowed, her brows furrowing a bit at the sight of a huge moving truck that had backed up into her new neighbor's driveway. On a trailer blocking the street was an old 59 Ford truck, navy blue. Next to that was a large older model black Cadillac with a gold grill.

She parked in front of the house happy she didn't have to try to squeeze by all of what was blocking the street. Although the moving truck was open and there was a ramp emerging from it, there was no one in sight. This pleased her as she was not feeling particularly sociable.

She switched off the truck's engine and registered the music blaring from inside the neighbor's garage. She sighed, hoping they would be cool and not stare at her once they found out she had been shot in the doorway of her roommate's house next door to them. She was so tired of being glared at all these weeks later.

Thoughts of him came swarming in again and the familiar pain of being abandoned stabbed at her heart. *No...nooooo...come on Peg, not today...* She tried to stop her mind from going to that place again. His face flashed before her, and tears threatened at the corners of her eyes. She squeezed them tight and took a deep breath. *No!*

She climbed out of the truck, slamming the door shut behind her as if that could help her to compartmentalize the memories.

It didn't work. She could feel her body begin to react from her legs up to her neck. Walking swiftly, she unlocked the front door and entered the house before making eye contact with anyone. She closed herself in her bedroom and leaned up against the door her breath erratic. Working out helped the cortisol in her body but thinking of Gunnar just brought it all rushing back.

Her bed called to her. She dumped everything in her hands on the floor, stepped out of her sneakers, and flopped onto her bed. This hurt her shoulder slightly, as it had only been five weeks since her surgery. *Five whole weeks.* Five weeks since he'd looked at her, said he loved her, and left the hospital room, disappearing and breaking her heart. He hadn't even stuck around to receive an award for saving her life and putting her ex in a psych ward for shooting and kidnapping her. *He saved her life and was gone.*

Tears fell onto her pillow. **When will this stop?** She felt the familiar shame and guilt for loving him so much. She didn't want to think of him in that way. She wanted to smile again. She wanted to remember all they had shared. The mind-blowing sex, the natural chemistry, the love...

Her phone buzzed. Part of Peg wanted to ignore it, leave it all the way across the room on the floor near her shoes. The other part of her knew it was her sister, Cady, who just landed back on the east coast. Cady had taken care of her for the last five weeks, four of which she'd spent trying to convince her to move back east with her.

Peg slid down the bed and crawled across the floor searching for the phone. Her clavicle hurt so she rolled over on her back and answered.

"Hey."

"Christ Pegasus Law, it took you long enough."

Peg smiled, wiping the tears away. "Sorry, I'm moving slow today. First day back at the gym since...*well...*"

"Oh, did you finally get there after dropping me at the airport?"

"Yes, but I spent a few hours sleeping first. How were your flights?"

Cady huffed. "Boring. I'll never understand why it takes two flights and seven hours to get from New Mexico to New Jersey."

"It's a fuel and money thing, Cad."

"Well, it wouldn't be an issue if you'd just stop being stubborn and leave Las Ramas, Peg. Asshole is put away, finally, so why don't you come home? I promise I'll be less annoying."

Peg smirked at the promise. However, she couldn't quite bring herself to tell Cady she couldn't leave her grandson or the man she loved more than any other. Part of her still hoped he'd come back to her.

"You're not annoying. My life is here; I can't just up and move back."

"Yes, you could, Peg. Let's change the subject so we don't argue."

"I'm not going to argue with you. I love you, please forgive me, you are right." Peg mocked her sister's favorite healing phrases.

"If that were true, you'd be here."

Peg chuckled, "I do love you, my sista!"

"I know. I meant the 'you are right part' bitch."

"Bitch."

Cady laughed. She loved how Peg could always keep up with her, "Alright. I need to go give my husband some attention. Just wanted to let you know I made it home. Thanks for driving me to the airport."

"Thanks for patching me up."

"I love you. Oh, they ever find that cop that saved you?"

13

"What?"

"The one that makes you do that...ask *'what?'*...and get sad when he's mentioned."

"Stop it, Cadmus."

"Okayyyy, I love you Peggers."

Peg's heart hurt again. "I love you more. Talk to you tomorrow."

She pushed the red button to end the call and let her hand fall to the floor. Her eyes searched the ceiling, but all she could see was his face, the way he'd look lovingly down at her as he entered her body making her breath hitch with his slow, sultry thrusts. He'd whisper to her and kiss her lips, telling her how tight her pussy was and how he couldn't get enough of her. She'd smile and move her hands down to his tush pulling him in deeper, tempting him to kiss her passionately. Peg sighed at the memories of their intense connection...the connection she couldn't seem to relinquish.

She rolled to her side, slid a hand under the bed and pulled out the journal she'd not written in since before being shot by Dereck. Writing was the only way she'd overcome PTSD she had. She knew it was going to hurt but she had to begin the long journey of trying to get over the greatest love she'd ever felt. Gunnar O'Clery had made the men before him in her life seem like a joke, but like them he'd loved her and left. The only way she'd ever gotten through heartbreak was writing it out. And here she was again, having to heal with her pen. She hoped she could.

Chapter 2
GUNNAR O'CLERY

Gunnar slowly drove down her street. Craning his head back, he could see her bedroom light was on. A mixture of relief and heartache suffused him. He hated having to leave for another couple of weeks. He was happy she was still in the same home; Dereck had been was put away; her sister had stayed; she'd healed.

He could leave town again, head up north for an indefinite amount of time on the case his boss was punishing him with. It had almost killed him to leave her, but she deserved better...he loved her enough to give her an opportunity to have a new life with someone who had something to offer her besides danger, stress, and loneliness.

He accelerated, trying not to feel the feeling deep sorrow and loss in his chest. He'd been trying to stay away...he wanted her so damn bad. He'd never fell for anyone the way he had for Peg, and now he had to help both of them forget. It was the right thing to do.

***

Chapter 3

UNDERSTAND

P eg clicked a pen and put it to the paper, hoping she could adequately express how she was feeling...in case he ever got a chance to read her thoughts. There were things she wanted him to know:

Peg's Journal Entry:

Gunnar,

I don't even know how to start. My sister left today and I'm lonely. I feel as if you've driven away and left me all over again.

See, I don't know why you left. How could you come into my life, pursue me, fuck me, make love to me, save me, visit me in hospital, tell me you love me...and leave? Please tell me what that was about? I don't understand. I'm trying not to blame myself but all you've left me with are my own thoughts.

No one seems to know what happened to you. When I called the station I was told you were away "on a case". You know I would never interfere with your work or try to find you if you didn't want that.

It's been weeks Gunnar. I don't know how to do this. How do I just forget all that we shared?

My feelings of abandonment are overwhelming. I'm surviving breath to breath, moment to moment. Time seems torturously slow. I can't understand how something that was so good, could feel so hurtful now.

Why is love feel so painful? You said you loved me, right?

I don't know where I'm going with this. I certainly don't want to be here lying on the floor, feeling sorry for myself. Pity is useless...just wasted moments.

I miss you.

I don't know how else to feel...I just miss everything.
I love you, Gunnar.

Josephine picked her cell up from her desk and began texting. She'd not heard from Peg in a week and knew it was time to tell her some things. Dereck was not letting up despite being put away by Gunnar, Aileen, and herself. Peg was *truly* loved. Gunnar had not only saved her life; he'd also made sure her ex was put away for good. Even Josephine couldn't figure out how he'd done it so fast, but he'd certainly made sure Dereck Law's file ensured he'd die in the psych hospital.

<u>Josephine's Cell</u>:
Hey you? Got time to hang out?

<u>Peg's Cell:</u>
Hi! That would be a welcomed treat yes. When?

Can you do Finley's at 7?

Sure can. See you then.

Peg got up from the floor wincing a bit from the soreness in her muscles. Getting back to the gym had helped emotionally but the weeks of sitting around recovering had made her feel as if she was starting from scratch.

She walked to her couch and sat down to check her phone messages. Six of her friends had been texting. Two were bugging her to set a date for the first women's group meeting she'd promised. She knew she had to nail down the place and time-she had put it off while recovering. They'd all heard about what had happened to he, and she was exhausted by the thought of having to explain it to them. She knew she needed the distraction though.

A few moments later she texted the owner of the shop she rented out of and secured the space to hold the meetings every week. Next, she sent a group chat informing the others about the particulars.

All she had to do was wait and the questions would come flooding in about what food to bring and how much wine was needed. She was already feeling drained. Standing and stretching, Peg reached for her keys and sunglasses. It was time to meet up with Josephine and vent. They'd formed a deep friendship in the last few months, and it was one she looked forward to nourishing.

Chapter 4
ARIZONA

Dereck stared out the window watching the sun go down. Another day passed. He scowled, looking around the room. Some patients had a card game going. A few were watching old episodes of Friends. Others were reading.

He hated the place. Hated the smell, the drab colors, hated all the different ages, but most of all he hated Gunnar O'Clery and how he'd played god-putting him here...*for her*.

He sunk down further against the back of the couch and vowed to get out and make sure they both paid for their actions against him-her for fucking Gunnar, and Gunnar for fucking him over and fucking...*her.*

He still could not believe the man who he'd wanted to be, the guy he'd fashioned is life after, who'd inspired the way he styled his truck and which guns he'd bought-the fucking SAME man-had taken his wife!

He leaned his head back, pursed his lips, and thought...***You're both going to pay.***

Aileen picked up on the second ring as her phone was sitting next to her on the couch. CNN was on the television with the sound muted.

"Yo! How you be, biotch?"

Josephine huffed a laugh, "Wow, she picks up on ring two AND is in a good mood? It must be my lucky fuckin' day."

"Oh stop. I'm always in a good mood."

"Yeah, okayyyyy. Listen, you wanna get out for a bit, maybe have a drink with Peg Law and I at Finley's?"

"You know I don't leave the house, Jo Jo."

"That's why I'm bugging you. Don't you want to get out? As your doctor, I'm recommending you socialize and get a change of scenery."

Aileen paused for a moment to consider it but thought better of trying to hobble around from a parking lot into a restaurant.

"I would love the gaze upon her beautiful face and that tight ass...but..."

"Stop. The girl is completely heartbroken. She needs your validation and kindness, not savage lesbianism Ai."

"He's still gone? Where did that motherfucker go? I can't believe he just disappeared after leaving her at the hospital. I'd never have believed him capable of that."

"He's probably on a case...overworking the way men do. He loves her; he's probably just having a hard time being okay with that." Josephine felt for them both, but mostly Peg. She really wanted them together.

"Sad. I tell ya, he's a great guy but always been his own island."

"Those are the best kind."

"Well, I hope he smartens up and returns to her. She's been through hell...he made that better but then left her. Hard."

Josephine agreed, "Hard for both of them. I mean he was trying to get out of a marriage; she was too. Hell, they're both still in the depths of divorce proceedings. One of the most tumultuous times in an adult's life is the transition from false love into the real thing."

"They did seem to have something real."

"They certainly did. So, I can't convince you to let me buy ya drinks and dinner, huh?"

"Nope, but, give her my best and let me know if she's wearing those thigh high leather boots with jeans."

"I will *not*...and you need to stop your shit."

"I refuse! Well behaved women rarely make history." Aileen let out a loud cackle.

Josephine rolled her eyes. "Ugh, you are incurable."

"True. Love ya. Have fun and be safe."

"Will do. Bye, Hoe."

"Bye...biotch."

Peg pulled out onto the highway. The hum of her truck's engine soothed her, and her mind slipped into thoughts of the last time they were together. She remembered how he backed her up against the bed, removed her clothing, and pressed his warm mouth against her most sensitive parts.

She'd cried out into the quiet of her room and he'd loved it. She'd reciprocated as she always had knowing that climbing onto him and letting his hard cock slide up and into her was his favorite. She'd slowly rocked and lulled them both with her slow tantric milking, loving how he whispered to her as she made his eyes roll back in his head. She knew when to stop, slide down, and blow him, bringing him to the edge only to climb back on him and coax him, over and over, until finally asking him to cum for her. He loved when she begged, even though she had all the control.

A car horn blared loudly, bringing Peg back to the present. She put her blinker on to exit the highway and head towards Finleys.

She had no idea how she would ever stop wanting him. Perhaps she never would.

Josephine was at the bar engaged in an intense conversation with the bartender. Peg could discern this because her friend's tush was off the bar stool as she leaned forward, laughing, pointing her finger at him while the other patrons giggled.

Peg sat down on the stool next to Josephine and waited. It only took a few moments.

"Oh my, there you are!" Josephine embraced her gently then looked into her eyes. "Does the shoulder hurt much Peg? Wow, I've missed you."

Peg felt good, finally. "Not too much. I've missed you too. What did I miss here? Sounds like a good time."

The bartender-a good-looking, twenty-something blonde-was waiting and staring at them both. A small grin played on his lips. He was young, muscular, and wearing a LRSU gray t-shirt, indicating he was probably half their age.

Josephine winked at him in her flirtatious way, "I'll have another one, baby. How about you, Peg? Are you drinking tonight?"

"Yes, please." She addressed the bartender. "May I have peach crown...uh, on the rocks."

He nodded and was off.

"Oh girl, you *are* drinking. Should have made it a double."

"I'm going slow but, yeah, it's been a long few weeks."

"Your sister was here, yes?"

"Yes, she went back to New Jersey today."

Josephine rubbed her good arm, "You doing okay?"

"Yeah." Peg shrugged slightly.

"Let's grab this booth over here." Josephine hopped down with her beer in hand and guided Peg as if she were fragile and in need of assistance.

"Sounds good. Don't fuss."

"Well, we can catch up without mister cutie eye-fucking us across the bar."

Peg laughed. She loved how Josephine's mind worked. She slid into the booth facing the door and Josephine sat across from her taking off her jean jacket and exposing all her colorful tattoos. Peg remembered her doing that at their first therapy sessions. She thought how nice it was to just be friends now and not have to race the clock to get everything out.

"Okay, so start where we left off the last time I called. Has asshole tried to contact you?"

Peg smirked. She knew she was referring to Dereck.

"No, thankfully. I heard he was a at the VA hospital in T or C?"

"Well, not exactly. Gunnar O'Clery had me and Aileen pull some strings and we had him moved to a psych ward in Scottsdale."

Peg's eyebrows raised, "In Arizona?"

"Yup."

"Oh my."

"Right? Gunnar is a sharp cookie. Had the motherfucker moved right near his mother so she could visit with him."

Peg's heart ached at the thought of Gunnar, his cleverness, his tact.

"Oh my god, Jo, Gunnar did to Dereck what Dereck did to his mother!"

"Genius, really. Dereck put his mother away only to have her taken out by his cousins. Now they can take his mother to visit him, and he can experience how she felt."

"He hates his family...*especially* his mother."

"Well now he can see how karma tastes. Gunnar doesn't play. He made a few phone calls, had me confirm some things and sign off on paperwork, and in the matter of a few days Dereck was drugged, transported, and living three hots and a cot in a psych ward seven hours away."

Peg was almost speechless. She'd had no idea. "I..."

"You have nothing to worry about now, other than what you're going to do with your house and your future. Gunnar even had Dereck's two dogs go to a good home...together."

Peg sat back and processed what she had been. told. The bartender brought her drink and Josephine's second beer. He lingered a moment, obviously trying to make eye contact, but left after realizing the two women were engaged in deep conversation.

"I can't believe this."

"What can't you believe, Peg? That you could get your house back? That you could go back to the life Dereck took from you? That a man could love you enough to see you get all the good you deserve? That he could want you to be happy after...well after you were shot and kidnapped?"

Peg's eyes began to fill with tears. "He saved my life."

"That he did...gallantly too."

"Yeah." Peg looked down into her glass, watching the ice cubes swimming in the brown whiskey.

"Listen, Peg, I know he's gone. I don't know where he went-hell not even Aileen knows where he is-but I do know that man loves you. And, well, men are men. Who knows what the fuck goes through their heads."

Josephine could see Peg was trying to be strong and hold back tears but abandonment and emotions were difficult to hide. She felt bad for her.

"That's intense coming from you," Peg said. "You work with people and their minds daily-"

"I will never profess to understand men. A man will fuck ten other women and still love just the one. They're complicated creatures yet we're supposed to be the difficult ones."

Peg huffed. "Well that doesn't make me feel better."

"I know. They are the strangest beings. He may have gone back to his wife Peg. You never know what sort of a hold she has over him. He has kids."

"Yes."

"That doesn't mean he doesn't love you; it doesn't mean he wouldn't save your life all over again. It's who he is as a man. He's full of faults like anyone...and fucked up too."

"It hurts so bad to be apart. I don't know how to..."

"What? Forget? You don't have to do that. No one knows the future. You do have the memories of what you both shared. Don't let that part go. Good memories should be treasured."

"I feel like I'm dying inside."

"We only feel pain if we feel loss. Your life is richer for it. Would you rather not have experienced the kind of love that most people can only dream of?"

Peg stared at her friend as she took in her words.

Josephine leaned back, her expression caring but nonchalant. "You know suffering is a choice, girl. What would happen if you chose differently?"

Peg looked from her to her glass. She sipped her drink and sighed.

"I know you're right, Jo. Thank you."

eg pulled up in front of the house and put the truck in park. She sat staring at the glow of the lights in the dashboard. Her mind wandered to the time Gunnar had admitted that, although he really enjoyed all the positions they fucked in, his favorite was when he could look into her eyes.

Peg hit the steering wheel with her palm trying to will away the stinging tears filling up her eyes. She couldn't get him out of her head.

She turned and looked at the house; she could see him walking into the house and into her room. She looked away and to the opposite side of the street. She recalled how he'd park his truck across from hers and how he'd hop down out of it, his holster and gun in his left hand, his phone in his right. She smiled remembering how he'd once crossed the street to her house while trying to cover his hard-on, after having texted, "I can't wait to be inside you.".

She took the keys out of the ignition and got out of the truck trying to wipe away tears. She's never wanted a man so much and he was still just *gone*.

Chapter 5

RICHIE HOLMES

Richie looked through the wooden blinds to see if Peg was home, but her truck was still gone. He'd been taking notice of Peg's comings and goings from her roommate's house next door. He'd only moved in a few days ago and although Las Ramas was not particularly eventful, watching her certainly was.

Dereck had never mentioned how much she'd changed since leaving him. She was stunning in her own way. Not overly done up, no designer clothing crap, just well groomed, thick, in shape, and blonde. Peg was the kind of woman who held herself well and made a man stare and wonder what could make her smile and look his way. He huffed, thinking how Dereck had really fucked up.

His eyes shifted toward movement; and he could see a young male in a wheelchair gliding around the corner on the sidewalk with two males about his age walking on either side of him. They stopped outside near the mailboxes, laughing at something. Richie decided it was time to be social and to try to get some information about what Peg had been up to since the incident. He headed out the door and pretended to check for mail.

"Hey!"

Richie waved to the three guys across the street from him and closed the lid to his mailbox. They stopped talking and waved back. He could see they were receptive to social overtures and that all three could be taken out with one swift kick of his six-three frame, so he trotted over to them and extended a hand to the one in the wheelchair first.

"Rich Holmes, how are you?"

"Matt Gantry. You just moved in, huh?"

Matt shook his hand making eye contact easier than his two companions.

"Yes, my son and I. He's at school still."

"This is Cam and Larsen."

Matt motioned toward each and they extended a hand mumbling a quick hello.

Richie could tell Matt was the more social of the three so he decided to engage with him.

"You all in high school?"

"No, I'm twenty. Gonna start a few college courses this semester. Cam is thinking about it, and Larsen works for his Dad at a dispensary on fifth."

"Oh okay. Ya'll into video games at all?"

"For sure. You?"

"I can hang, when my kid lets me, but mostly I work from home. Analyst for the base."

Matt's eyebrows raised. He knew that meant Rich was...well rich. However, he was curious as to why he was living in their development when most like him chose to live up the mountain.

"Oh, so, fed?"

"Something along those lines. So, what can you tell me about the neighborhood here? Everyone seems pretty decent so far."

"Well, who have you met?" Larsen spoke in a low tone of voice. His oily black hair hung in front of one eye.

Richie looked across the street at Peg's place then turned to them, "Well, so far-"

"Ah, you've met Peg Law?"

Matt smiled wide. Richie didn't have a chance to answer.

"The most beautiful woman in Legends East!" Cam piped up enthusiastically.

Larsen mumbled, "She was shot."

"What the fuck, Larsen? Grow a filter would ya?" Matt squinted at his friend.

"Oh, sorry."

Richie observed their body language as Matt tensed his arms and Larsen stepped away from his wheelchair.

"Oh, really?"

Richie was curious as to how much they know. He waited and looked at Matt who obviously liked Peg and wanted to explain.

"Yeah, well her ex shot her in that doorway right there. Not sure she would want anyone to know, but this knucklehead is a blabbermouth." Matt jutted a thumb toward Larsen who piped up again.

"Then he took her, ya know? He kidnapped her but the cops got her back before he killed her."

Larsen rocked on his heels a little too close to Matt who took the opportunity to jerk his wheelchair forward and knock him in the shin.

"Shut your hole, Larsen!"

"Ouch fucker!" Larsen swung purposely over Matt's head, obviously not wanting to hit him in his chair.

Richie fought back the urge to laugh. The trio reminded him of three characters on 3rd Rock from the Sun.

"That's very frightening but I'm glad it worked out. Don't worry, I won't say anything. I'm sure that's not something she would want all the neighbors knowing."

Matt shrugged. "She probably doesn't, but, unfortunately, they all do. She moved there trying to stay away from her crazy-ass ex, but he found her. She's safe now because he's been put away."

"But now we're sad because she'll go back to her big house on the west side, and we won't get to see her wave to us anymore," Cam's nasal voice bellowed.

Richie wondered if he had a hearing problem or was partially deaf in one ear.

"Oh I see." He was not too happy to hear she would be moving back to the house so soon. He'd just moved in. Luckily, it was a month-to-month Airbnb situation.

Matt looked somber as he said, "It'll be a sad day on this street when Pegasus Law leaves. She's the best neighbor we've ever had."

"Pegasus Law? Wow, that's the first time I've ever heard of that name." Richie lied.

"It's as magical as her." Larsen said.

"I'm going to thwart you, Larsen." Matt gave his friend a threatening look.

Richie fought back laughter again, "Well guys it was nice to-"

Music blared from her truck as Peg turned onto the street. She pulled up in front of her roommate's house and parked in her usual spot. She noticed the Escalade in front of her truck and looked around. To the left she saw the four men staring at her.

Part of her thought she should pretend to be on a call and briskly walk up the driveway and into the house but the more sociable part of her thought better of it. She'd heard the boys had been helpful in guiding Gunnar when she had been taken. The tall

30

new neighbor was with them too and she was admittedly curious about him. She opened the door and hopped down. Her thigh high boots landing surprisingly balanced, she waved, shut the door and walked towards them noticing the three younger boys wide-eyed and not talking.

Her eyes found her new neighbor's and he softened, a small smile reaching the corners of his mouth.

Richie watched her as she walked confidently and gracefully towards them, not looking like someone who'd recently been shot.

"Evening." Her voice was low and melodious. Richie felt it in his loins.

"Good evening. How are you?"

Peg lifted her hand towards him, and he let her slide it long and soft into his grasp. "Peg. Welcome to the neighborhood."

"Richie Holmes. Thank you. I've been warmly received so far."

Her eyes danced and she smiled, her beautiful teeth peeking out from her perfect shade of lipstick. Richie thought for a moment how her nipples might be the same shade.

She slowly drew back her hand and used it for a casual wave. "Hey guys, how's it going?"

"Good." Matt formulated the word while Cam and Larsen grunted in unison.

Peg looked from them back to Richie. "Are you enjoying Las Ramas so far?"

"I'm settling in. Moved here from Texas with my fifteen-year-old son, RJ."

"Oh, great. Work-related?" She was guessing.

Richie nodded. "Work, divorce...helping out Mom-that sort of stuff."

The three boys looked up at him as he shared way more with her than he had with them.

"Oh, I see. She lives here?" She looked over at his house.

"No. She's in the historic district but needing more help these days. I'm trying to convince her I have plenty of room, but she's the sort that needs to think it's her idea."

It wasn't a total lie. He'd just left out the part about her ex calling in his favor to him and how he was supposed to watch her while Dereck figured out how to get out of the psych ward in Arizona that her lover had him put in. Meeting her now was making him wonder if he wanted to help Dereck at all. She seemed very different than he'd described. Lovely...in a way that was comforting.

Peg laughed. "I know what you mean."

Richie watched her chest move and thought how he'd love to make her laugh more to see if she crinkled her nose or turned red. He thought she was stunning.

"Oh, you have a mom like that?"

"Hyper-independent? Yep, but she's all the way on the East Coast the way I like it."

He smiled. "Ah, gotcha."

Peg looked from him to the boys who were staring. "So what's new guys? Seen anything crazy lately?" She winked, teasing them.

Matt spoke up before one of his idiot friends could, "Not lately, Ms. Law. Not even Lieutenant O'Clery." Matt's mouth clamped shut as he realized how stupid he had been.

She forced herself to smile as if hearing the name didn't hurt deep down.

"Well, Rich Holmes, it was a pleasure. I should get inside; I hear my bed calling me."

"It's Richie...I mean, everyone calls me *Richie.*"

"Oh, okay, well nice meeting you, welcome, and you know where we live if you're needing a cup of sugar or an egg. My roommates are pretty decent. Just push the button on the ring camera."

Richie smiled lifting his large hand in a small waving gesture. "Thanks. It was great meeting you."

Peg turned to give the younger men a nod, "Gentlemen."

All four said goodbye and watched her cross the road appreciating how snugly her jeans fit her in all the right places. She knew she would be talked about after she was gone, but she was past caring. What she really wanted to do was get into bed and dream of all Gunnar had done to her there.

After sliding into silk pajamas, Peg got under the covers and took her journal out. She knew if she didn't write it would take too long to finally get to sleep. Every hour she was sleeping was an hour she didn't have to miss him, so getting sleepy while penning some thoughts was a must.

Peg's Journal Entry:

Today, as I was going about my day, I realized my thoughts are heavy with the memories of us. I even met a new neighbor and spent time around other men, but I don't feel one ounce of attraction to anyone else.

Gunnar is my person. I miss his smell, his voice, the way he purses his lips right before his dimples appear. I want him so much I ache in places I didn't even know existed in my body.

While I was driving today, I recalled the time he was fucking me in missionary. He slowed down then eventually stopped, to say, "You know I'm in love with you, right?"

I'll never forget what my heart did. It was as if my heart and mind wanted to battle. I knew I loved him, years back, but I'd never admitted it. Like a dummy I fell silent and stared at him in disbelief.

I mean there was one time he'd said "love ya" as he was ending a call but I'd brushed it off as if it was an accident and something he did with his kids.

I stared and stared. He was looking down at me, his dick still rock-hard inside me. My body wanted to caress and milk him but I was frozen in time.

I wanted to tell him I'd loved him for years, but my mouth wouldn't move because every time I had admitted my love to a man, he'd left me. Of course, what I'd felt for others was nothing in comparison to how intensely I loved Gunnar. In fact, my relationships before him seem like a joke-silly, childish, desperate love-whereas he felt like home-like a love I'd waited for my whole life.

Finally, he glanced away and softly said, "You don't feel the same, do you? It's ok..."

"I do though. I've loved you for..."

I remember choking up, the admission stuck in my throat, my heart aching because he had said it first and I wanted to let the flood gates open and all my truth run out. I wanted the relief...but if I told him everything he would leave. My brain screamed YOU LOVE HIM! BUT IF YOU TELL HIM HE MAY RUN LIKE THE OTHERS! I remember wanting to squeeze the negativity out.

"Are you crying?"

I couldn't answer. The lump in my throat was choking me.

He leaned in and kissed me. I kissed him back and he started slowly thrusting inside me. I met him at each torturously pleasurable movement. He kissed me deeper, sliding in further to make love to my body...my soul.

He stopped. "When did you know?"

"When did you?" I whispered, finally able to look at his beautiful brown eyes again.

"About six months ago. You?"

"I think years back when you shook my hand...but that day you showed up at the laundromat to hug me...that was when my body relented. I caught your scent, felt your energy when you scooped me into that embrace. I knew then...I'll never not...love this man... I'm scared Gunnar."

He kissed me deeper and made love to me until I eased. I'm still scared. How do I do this? How do I live in a world where he is out there...and I'm here just loving him...

Peg's hand stopped writing. The journal flopped onto her lap and the pen fell as she lay her head back on her pillow, trying to will away the tears. Her heart hurt so bad. She wanted to remember everything, but every memory felt like a knife to the heart. She rolled to her side letting everything fall to the floor. Reaching up she turned the light off and settled into the darkness of the room where they'd shared so much with each other.

Chapter 6

HER

Gunnar tossed and turned. She was, again, heavy in his thoughts and his cock was not cooperating. He needed to get to sleep so he could deal with the new parameters of the case in the morning, but he wasn't feeling the least bit tired.

His thoughts moved to her again. This time he didn't fight it. He closed his eyes and suddenly he could see her. She was wearing her black heels; her legs splayed open; lacy lingerie complimented her tan skin; her chest rose and fell as she breathed heavily with the arousal she had for him. Wet and wanting. She always made him feel as if he were the only man for her.

He remembered touching her gently, with one hand on her beautiful round breast, the other trailing down her tummy to her most sacred area. She arched towards his hand, and he slid two fingers into her. She was like velvet-warm and slick. He pressed in deeper, his thumb finding her clit. A breathy moan escaped her tantalizing mouth, and her head fell back onto the pillow as he began to swirl slowly and push further in, finger-fucking her gorgeous pussy.

She was so wet. As he continued to slowly pleasure her, he could feel her arousal squirting out, lubricating his fingers and dripping down to his palm. He loved the feel of her. Every part of his engorged cock wanted to be inside her.

He started removing his clothing with his free hand, all the while watching her writhe in pleasure, her hands grasping at the wrought iron headboard. Her body called to him, her legs falling open.

He climbed on top of her and pushed into her tight wetness. Her arms came around him and she pulled his muscular ass into her. She loved his thrusts and rewarded him by clenching him tight while sinking her mouth into his neck. Shivers of bliss traveled through his entire body and he wanted to whisper into her ear how much he loved her...

Peg's eyes suddenly opened for no reason. She sighed. She wanted him so badly her body ached, and her mind screamed out for him. She pressed her head into the pillow, squeezing her eyes shut, as if it could help her avoid her thoughts. It wasn't helping. All she could see was him...how he would touch her and run his fingers along her skin, down over her breasts and stomach. He would wrap his strong hands around her hips and pull her in to his body, pressing his erection into her and moaning softly in her ear to let her know how much he wanted her. She'd never felt more desired.

A memory flashed in, and she allowed it. He'd called while she was out having dinner with GeeGee. She'd had trouble sleeping that night because she missed him so much and was excited to feel him inside of her again. He'd texted "want you" by 8:30 a.m., then, by 9:30 a.m., he'd walked into her room, stopping a moment to look at her on the bed, in awe of her.

His breath hitched as she gazed at him over her shoulder. She was on her stomach, wearing heels, her legs bent, her tan butt peeking out from her black thong...her blonde hair cascading down her back.

He'd whispered, "Don't move", and disrobed, throwing his shirt and workout pants on the floor as he'd made his way to her, gently climbing up behind her. He'd pressed his hard cock between her thighs and sunk his mouth down into the curve of her neck. Peg gasped in surrender, and he'd moaned, loving the sound of her throaty exhale. His sucking and nibbling at her soft skin had made her instinctively arch up into him, her vulva slick with evidence of her desire for him to enter her from behind.

As if hearing her body begging, Gunnar had reached down, running a finger along her thong and moving it to the side to push the head of his cock into her wet, warm, slickness. He'd exhaled and paused at the feeling o her body embracing his. He loved how tight her pussy always was. Every time they'd been together, she was tight. The initial entry always took a few slow, long thrusts despite how soaked she'd get. He never tired of that moment and often dreamed of her accepting him into her body when they were apart. She always accepted him, always arched towards him pushing back to meet all of him and his entire length inside her. Nothing felt better in the world than Peg wanting him.

He'd pushed again and she'd pressed back to him...*again*. He'd loved how she fucked and made love to him. Her every movement was intentional and energetic. No woman had ever made him feel so free and captivated. Peg was the most magnificent lover he'd ever experienced.

She'd reached forward grabbing the rungs of her headboard moaning in ecstasy at how he was pleasuring her body. He'd loved the way her body reacted to him; she was raw and honest in her lovemaking, and often she'd grasp for the walls or bed, or sheets, or him as if trying to grab onto the earth. She'd always flowed and matched his rhythm and energy perfectly and her breathing had been intense. He'd known it was why she could cum so much. Sex to her was art...*their* art. She'd been totally committed. A true tantrica.

Gunnar slid out of her and quietly turned her over. His mouth had come down between her legs and he'd parted her with his soft lips. She'd cried out at the sensation and arched up to let him sink deeper into the pleasure apex of her body. He'd swirled his tongue and sucked at her clit, sending surges of pleasure through her entire body letting her orgasm build. He'd spread her open wider, tongue-thrusting slow and torturously as she cried out his name.

He'd loved her breathlessness and the sound of his name from her mouth. He'd been able to feel her trying to prolong her orgasm and instead he'd stopped and said, "cum for me baby". He'd lowered his mouth again and picked up their rhythm, forcing her over the cliff. Her body had convulsed and writhed in shuddering bliss, her head lifted up as she cried out again, making him feel like a god. He loved pleasuring her.

Just when she'd started to catch her breath, he'd pulled her hips to the edge of the bed, thrusting his engorged cock full and deep into her dripping pussy. He'd loved the way she felt after she came and watching her begin to gain strength again, pressing to him and squeezing him inside her. She was a sexual goddess. He'd looked down at her beautiful face and body, thrusting deep, trying not too cum just yet.

"You...were intense last week..." He'd continued to pull her hips to him as he flexed his pelvis towards her. He'd pointed to the area above his right nipple and Peg had seen the endings of a yellowish bruise.

"Remember...you sunk your mouth into me...*and bit me*."

Breathless, she tried to reply, "I'm...I'm. So sorry...I-"

"Don't apologize; I liked it. You wanted me."

"I always want you."

"Who's pussy is this?"

Peg smiled, "Only yours. My body only wants you, baby."

"Mmmmm...you make me so happy."

Gunnar had reached forward, placing his hands on her breasts, caressing her as he'd continued to thrust slowly in and out.

Peg had run her fingernails gently down his large pecs, "I love how you touch me, Gunnar."

"Mmmm...." He'd wanted to reward her again. He pulled out of her and moved down her body. He'd kissed, sucked, and flicked his tongue in various combinations to help her orgasm build. He'd loved how multi-orgasmic Peg always was and took his time pleasuring all of her, so she'd always had another one coming. He'd felt a deep satisfaction that he could always please her.

Standing up again, he'd opened her legs wider, sliding deep inside. Peg had gasped, watching him as he looked down staring at how beautiful her pussy looked with him, long and hard, moving in...and out of it.

"Jesus, you're beautiful, Peg. You should see what I get to see."

Peg had smiled, "I like my view too."

His eyes had met hers and she'd reached forward, motioning for him to kiss her mouth. He'd come down onto his forearms and given her what she was asking for, the weight of him making her want him more. She'd opened her mouth and he'd deepened the kiss, their bodies still moving in perfect rhythm together.

Peg's eyes opened as the visuals disappeared and headlights shone into her room, moving along the walls. She couldn't believe how immersed she'd been in the memories of their exquisite connection. She'd never felt such attraction for another man. She sighed, trying not to feel sorrow. Her eyes drifted shut and she allowed her body to sink down into the mattress. Suddenly her cell dinged. She reached for it and saw it was her roommate.

<u>Rena's Cell:</u>
Peg are you awake?

<u>Peg's Cell:</u>
Yes...you okay?

Some guy is at the door asking for you. I can see him through the camera.

Oh shit. I'm sorry. Let me see what's going on.

K

Peg threw the covers to the side, grabbed her gun, and went to the front door. She knew it wasn't Dereck, so anyone else was less of a threat. She hoped it was Gunnar but didn't allow herself to expect too much. He would have texted first, knowing she'd not appreciate surprises, especially after what she'd been through.

She looked through the peephole and saw it was the new neighbor. His face was pleasant and his body language relaxed. She decided to open the door a crack but kept her gun close to her belly just in case. Craning her neck around, she peeked through the opening at him.

Richie's eyebrows raised and he smiled. "Hey...uh hi Peg, I'm so sorry to bother you. My mother fell in her home, and I had to have her taken to the ER. I hate to ask but I don't know many other residents on our street yet. Do you think you could keep an eye on my house while I meet her at the hospital? My son is asleep, and I have two dogs to protect him but...well, just in case. I hate leaving him as he's underage."

"Oh...uh-"

"I'm sorry, that was quite a mouthful at ten o'clock in the evening."

Peg tried to smile, her eyes not quite focused yet. "No no, of course. I mean uh...does he know you've left?"

"I texted him, but he's asleep and I don't want to wake him. May I leave him your number in case he needs anything?"

Peg looked down at her phone, "Oh, yeah of course. What's your number first? His name?"

"Area code nine one nine, three five six, seven three seven three. His name is RJ."

Peg smiled, "Of course it is." She typed in his number and sent him a text.

"I know, real original right?"

"Actually yes. Okay, there, I've sent you a message, so you have my number."

"Thank you so much. I am truly sorry to bug you. I'll text you his number as well."

"No worries. Let him know my name and that I'm here if he needs anything." She smiled not knowing how she could help the kid, but it was her nature to be empathic.

"I'll text him. If I don't make it back in the morning I'll have him call an Uber to get a ride to school, so he'll only be home until seven thirty or so. He's pretty independent."

"Most teens are these days. Does he need a ride to school?"

"I can't put you out like that. I just need an eye on him while I deal with my mom. Pretty sure she broke her hip. You know how older folks get."

Peg nodded. "True. I hope she's not in too much pain."

42

"Thank you and I appreciate this, Peg. I know I just met you, but we literally moved in only a few days ago so I only know you and well...the Matt guy in the wheelchair and his friends so...I think you're my best bet."

"Right. I get your concern."

"Okay, I don't want to keep you any longer...and please tell your uh...well, I'm sorry to have disturbed you all." Richie looked into the doorbell camera and waved.

"Oh yes, sorry, Rena." Peg talked a bit louder to apologize to her roommate, who had heard the whole conversation and now knew there was a new neighbor with a kid next door.

Richie stepped back and looked over at the hole in the metal screen door. He wondered if it was related to the shooting. His eyes reverted back to hers. "I'll go now. Thank you so much. I really appreciate your help."

"You're welcome."

"Okay. Bye."

Peg closed the door and headed back to her dark room. Her cell dinged in her hand as she holstered her gun at her bedside.

Rena's Cell:
Whoa

Peg's Cell:
So sorry

That's the new neighbor? He's hot!

Lol, you're funny.

He seems to trust you, as most of us do.

43

Ty, not sure what I can do to help but I've had issues like that before when my kids were small and had to ask my neighbor for help.

Me **too. It's good to have decent ones.**

Were you asleep?

Not really. He's big!

Very tall.

Kinda yeah. I bet he likes you.

Stop. I just met him earlier today. I guess he doesn't know many people on our street yet.

True. I only like the neighbors to our left, everyone else keeps away.

Well...yeah.

Not because you were shot, they kept away before your ex went bonkers.

Lol. So glad that's over.

So glad you're safe! I'll let you get back to dreaming.

How'd you know?

I've seen the men that come to your door girl Who wouldn't dream of them? Well except for that fat crazy ex of yours. Lol.

You kill me (laughing emoji)

Nite roomie.

Nite.

Peg slid into her bed, her mind racing but not in the ways she'd hoped. Despite her low expectations, she'd still felt immense disappointment when she'd opened the door and not seen Gunnar. She snuggled beneath the covers, tried to settle her heart, and closed her eyes...hoping he would return to her, if not in reality, at least in her dreams.

Chapter 7
MAGIC

Gunnar opened one eye and tapped the screen of his phone on the nightstand. It was only three o'clock in the morning. He rolled his eyes and turned over, annoyed that he'd only been asleep for a few hours. His dick hitched beneath the sheet as he thought of her again. ***Damn it, O'Clery.*** He could not get her out of his head...or his heart. Even with all the stress of his divorce and the new apartment, the new bed...he could not distract himself enough to heal from her.

He opened his eyes and stared up at the ceiling, wondering if he should just get up and shower. His dick was rock-hard despite him trying to redirect his thoughts. It wasn't working.

He closed his eyes again and there she was. He pictured the curve of her body as she lay on her stomach on the bed. He missed how she would wear black lingerie and heels for just for him. He thought of the time he'd walked in her room and told her not to move. He remembered climbing on top of her gorgeous body, spreading her legs, moving her thong aside and sliding into her tight, wanting pussy. She was always so tight but ready. Peg was always wet for him, and it made him feel incredibly desired. It was as if she had been made just for him.

He couldn't resist reaching a hand down to touch himself. He remembered how she'd touched him, how her mouth would engulf his shaft and her tongue would tantalize his head. He loved how she would move slowly up and down his length and twist her palm around his base in perfect rhythm with her tongue and lips. She would even lick and suck his balls, one at a time and kiss the insides of his thighs if she felt him get close. Peg knew how to prolong pleasure in her tantric ways. He ached for her and missed her so fucking much.

Drifting off again he could see her in his mind, her mouth moving up and down on him as he'd held her hair back. He'd adored how'd she'd kiss up his stomach, spend time on each of his nipples until he could stand no more, then slide down on his cock all the way to the base.

She'd begin her slow rocking and sensual thrusts, making sure to clench around him each time she lifted up, moving his shaft skin along his stiff cock. She called it "milking" and no woman had ever fucked him like that. It had almost driven him mad, and when she'd seen his eyes begin to glaze over, she'd pick up the pace and fuck him into oblivion.

He'd grasp her hips and spill his cum inside her, holding his breath. She'd always bend down and whisper in his ear, "Breathe, baby...b r e a t h e..." and coax him into the most magnificent orgasms he'd ever experienced.

She had been the most exquisite lover, and as he pleasured himself to the thought of all she'd done to him, he exploded under the sheets, his chest heaving...and his heart aching for her. *Oh Peg baby, I love you...I...*

Gunnar's whispers brought him back to the room and he looked around realizing she wasn't there.

Richie Holmes waited as the phone rang a third time. A voice came on the line, and he cleared his throat.

"Psych Unit, Clara speaking."

"Hi Clara. I was patched through for patient D. Law. Is he available?"

"Let me ring the hall phone and see if he's nearby. Who is asking?" Clara picked up a pen to scribble on her pad of paper.

"It's Reynaldo, his cousin."

"Oh, okay Reynaldo, I'll try to get him. Hold, please."

She placed him on hold as some funky elevator type music played low in the background. He waited, spinning a fidget spinner his kid gave him. Dereck was not his favorite person, but he did owe him. He leaned back against his mother's couch and stretched his long legs out letting the blood flow better.

He thought of Peg and how pretty she was. Dereck had really fucked up. Not only did he lose a really great wife to Las Ramas' top cop, but he also botched the kidnapping, shot her, and got fucking dumped in a mind tank for life.

He heard the line pick up. "Yo bra-" Dereck sounded chipper and not as drugged as the last time he'd called.

"Hey, cuz. How ya holding up?" Richie didn't like pretending they were cousins, but he knew, most likely, that the line was not secure and that they only let him talk to family and his lawyer.

Dereck was relieved to hear from Richie and proud that he'd cheeked and spit out his afternoon meds so he was more coherent.

"How is she?"

"You didn't mention how hot she was, Dereck, what the fuck?"

"Don't fuck her unless you have to, man. So, you moved in and all?"

"I'm all moved in. She's with my kid, man...well, not exactly. I'm at my mom's and asked her to keep an eye on him. She thinks Mom fell and that I'm at the hospital. I feel bad lying to her. She's way nicer than I thought."

"No, she's not, Richie. Is *he* anywhere near her?"

"No. I haven't seen any visitors yet, but I've only been in the neighborhood a week. What's the plan?...and remember, I'm only returning a favor for how you helped me get divorced from Jana. Don't ask me for more than that."

Richie was feeling like shit already for agreeing to help Dereck. Peg was not the bitch Dereck had said she was...at least not so far. He could have mentioned her appearance and how admired she is by others in the neighborhood.

Dereck felt annoyed. He needed to figure out how to get Richie to hate Peg, but with limited contact and phone calls he knew he couldn't adequately brainwash him as he needed to. This could be risky. Peg was easily loved by others.

"I just need you to get to know her better but NOT TO FUCK HER. Let me know when she starts to pack up and move back into my house. I want to know if he helps her or moves in with her. It's only a matter of time before her asshole lawyer has her back in the home and convinces her to take over all I setup. I can't believe the bitch got it all."

"It is half hers, man."

"Shut the fuck up."

"Don't talk to me that way, Dereck. I'm trying to help you here."

"Then do that. I don't need you telling me my shit is half hers."

Richie rolled his eyes. "Did you find out if it was her that got you transferred to that hospital?'

49

"Apparently, O'Clery pulled strings with the help of an old counselor we'd had. I can't get anyone to listen to me. Even my VA lawyer is trying to convince me to let this go, but dude, I'm going crazy in here."

Richie raised his eyebrows, "Well bud, you did shoot and kidnap her. The psych ward is a lot better than prison for attempted murder, right? I mean, at least you're not getting butt-fucked every night."

"That won't be happening here. With all the drugs they sling it's a wonder anyone can even find their own dick."

Richie ignored the comment and tried not to think about Dereck's genitals, especially since they'd been in his ex-wife, which helped him get divorced as planned.

"Good. Okay, so I'll just continue on with watching her for you. I'll call you next week with an update."

Dereck grunted. "Uh huh, yeah...and Ri- err, Reynaldo?"

"Yeah, cuz."

"Don't fuck her."

Richie laughed. "You mean the way you did my ex?"

"That was for your own good, man. I told you she was embezzling. I had to get you to pay attention to her character. Aren't you happier now...and richer?"

"Yes...but still."

"I'm telling you, do NOT fuck her. She has magic in her and the tightest pussy. Look what she did to O'Cler...err my friend."

Richie huffed, "I don't think he thought of you as a friend, Dereck. Look where you are."

"Whatever man, just...don't get too close to her. I'm telling you...you'll fall in love and fuck everything up. You owe me."

Chapter 8

IN PERSON

Josephine walked from one patient room to the next texting Aileen:

Josephine's Cell:
So you haven't found him or you're not trying? Her heart is in pieces Ai she is so sad.

Aileen's Cell:
Not trying Jojo. He's on a case. I'm not going to research the guy if he doesn't want to be found. I do know his wife filed for divorce last month but word is, she cheated on him and he found out. He's probably moving and such or happy to be on a case away from his personal life stuff. He's protecting her by staying out of her life.

But he loves her, I know he does. I can feel it. You know how I am about my gut feelings. And...she is so in love with him. They belong together. Life is fucking short!

I'm sure they love each other but there's nothing we can do about that.

We helped them before

That was different. Her crazy ex was after her.

Still...shouldn't there be a happily ever after Ai?

That rarely happens with these law enforcement types.

I want it to in this case. They are both great people...and soooo fucking hot.

I agree. It's just none of our business woman!

This town needs a good story...can you imagine the power couple they'd be?

Get your head out of your ass doc. Don't you have patients to see...or you at your counseling office today?

I'm at urgent care today. Got a dude with a boil on his left ass cheek. I'd much prefer to help Peg.

You're heart is in the right place but we have to leave this one up to fate.

Killjoy

That's me. Kisses-

A ileen laid her head back against the pillow, put aside her cellphone, and used the remote to change the channel. She was curious as to where Gunnar O'Clery had disappeared to. Her contact at LRPD told her he'd gone on a case while Peg was still in the hospital and that his boss was not too happy about how things went down with Dereck Law. It had been quietly taken care of.

She's was almost sure his already failing marriage had crumbled beyond repair once his ex found out about Peg. It seemed he was supposed to forgive her indiscretions, raise her kids, but he wasn't afforded the same courtesy in return.

Aileen shook her head knowing that infidelity was the kiss of death in a relationship. You could forgive and try to move on but you could never go back to the same relationship. A whole new one had to be invented.

She knew that the man loved Peg. Who wouldn't? He was probably just trying to figure out how *not* to. She whispered into the air, "Good luck, bud...just surrender and be happy. Love doesn't visit everyone. You may have something that lasts... foreverrrrr..."

Gunnar woke, she *still* on his mind. He couldn't believe he'd fallen back to sleep! He jumped up and rushed to the shower, wishing she were already in there waiting for him. He'd love to see the hot water run down along her back, creating goosebumps along her beautiful body. He'd kiss them all and help her relax.

Peg stood out on the walkway near the door, her scrubs on, makeup and hair freshly done, a cup of tea steaming in her hand. She watched RJ walk down his driveway, his long legs showing through skinny jeans, a black book bag hiked up on one shoulder, his long brown hair wet on his back.

He looked over his shoulder and waved at her as he opened the door of his waiting Uber. She waved back. She thought he was as attractive as his father, albeit smaller.

She hoped he was off to school as she watched over him as promised. Reaching down, she searched for her cell in her shirt pocket and quickly took a photograph of him and the car before it drove off. Although she'd never met RJ, she still wanted to let his father know she'd seen him leave for school on time.

Peg's Cell:
Hello Richie?

Richie's Cell:
Good morning Peg.

RJ is off to school...I hope? (Pic sent of car and license plate)

Oh great, ty!

How's your Mom?

Oh, she's only got a big bruise. Already back home getting her settled in. Can I thank you with lunch?

Can't gotta see clients. But thanx.

Dinner then...a drink? I'm a good cook.

I'll think about it. Got a full day. Glad today is better for you. You good with RJ now?

I'll pick him up yes. Thanks again neighbor. You're amazing.

Lol, have a good one.

***

Peg's Journal Entry:
Life has been strange for me lately. I got back into working today and my shoulder is sore as fuck but at least I can work. I notice I am calmer riding around and working downtown now that Dereck is in Arizona. I don't know how Gunnar and Josephine pulled it off, but I am so grateful. I feel I can move forward with my business and finally getting back into my house.

I have yet to go over to the house, I can't even imagine what he's done to it. I've been trying to muster the strength to put myself through all

54

the memories. I think I just want to make new ones, even if that means selling all the old along with the house.

I met the new neighbor here and literally a few hours later he was knocking on our door for me to keep an eye on his fifteen-year-old son next door while he met his mother to the ER. So strange. He doesn't know anyone else on the street, so I was the go-to person. He's kind of attractive in a tall dad-bod guy kind of way. It's nice to have one person in the neighborhood that doesn't look at me as the "lady that was shot by her ex" but I know he'll be told of my drama, if he hasn't already been.

I am missing Gunnar terribly. I don't know how to let it all go...if I'm even supposed to do that. The intimacy we had and the passion we shared was so intense, I honestly don't know what to do with the memories or where to put them. I find myself thinking of him almost every few minutes. I can't un-hear his words as he left my hospital room, and my mind and body can't seem to grasp that he just...disappeared. I hope he's okay. I'm trying to keep my spirits up, but my mind can't seem to come to terms with having been abandoned again. Why is it men can love me, but they can't choose me? What is it about me that makes them leave?

Chapter 9
REMEMBER

eg tossed and turned, unable to evade the visuals. Half asleep and yet falling in and out of dreaming she could feel him close. Perhaps he was thinking of her at the same time she was thinking of him.

Her mind wandered. She could sense him, smell his fresh scent again. Sighing she turned and settled on her back, her eyes glaring at the ceiling in the dark for a moment. Her eyelids felt heavy, and she closed them once again as the visions flooded in. He was there again in her room...stepping towards her, taking her in his arms.

I remember us Gunnar...our first time...I...remember:

I looked up at you, my knees weak with want for you to touch all of me. It had been so long since I'd been touched by a man, and even longer since I'd felt this much desire for one. I wanted you.

The low chatter of your radio communication reminded both of us that you were still clothed. You stepped back, gazing down at my face then my body. You pulled off your gun-belt, and laid it down across the room near the wall. I watched at how you unfastened your bulletproof vest and moved it over your head to lay it down next to the belt. I felt somewhat nervous and exposed, so I walked around the room, preparing the bed, wondering what we would do first, excited you wanted me.

You continued to disrobe, taking off your shoes, shirt, pants, placing everything to the side while whispering how beautiful you felt I was. I couldn't help my smile or keep my hands from excitedly reaching out to help you with your remaining layers.

I remember getting incredibly wet as you revealed more and more skin. I had no idea how beautiful you were underneath your uniform! I was intensely excited you were about to share your body with me.

My gaze trailed down your thick neck to your broad chest. Your pecs were beautifully sculpted and moved into tight, washboard abs and then to a tiny waist, maybe all of thirty-two inches, if that. I liked your overbuilt lats and incredibly large biceps, which I wanted to run my hands down and linger over.

My body responded suddenly with aching and yearning at the sight of your erect cock. You walked to me to embrace me and remove my last piece of clothing. Feeling your arms around me and the warmth of your strong hold solidified that I wanted nothing more than that moment. I could feel you had to have me and was amazed that you were even in my room only eleven hours after kissing me for the first time!

Before I knew it, you were lying back on my bed, pulling me to you.

"Come here, baby...." You whispered gruffly, and I swear I pulsed inside at the sound of your desire for me.

Explosions were going off in my brain as my body tingled all over. I wanted you so badly. This being only the second time I'd seen you in over ten years, made everything so new and exciting, yet you felt like home.

Your body, rippled with taut muscle, felt so good under my hands. Your chest was huge as you pulled me close, your hands playing along and down my body.

"You look so beautiful in this low lighting...", you hummed melodiously in my ear.

You watched me smile and then lower my face, making my way towards your cock with my mouth. I placed it softly over your glazed head, your precum warm on my tongue.

You inhaled, "Ohhhhh myyyyy...baby..."

I moaned, enjoying the way you tasted. As I continued my slow assault, I noticed my mouth was a bit snug for your large size but I continued to lubricate you as you squirmed, moaning in ecstasy. I slowly moved my lips and tongue down farther over your shaft. You were bigger than I'd expected, but I liked it.

You sucked in air through your teeth at the pleasure of finally feeling my mouth on you. I reached my palm around your cock, moving your soft skin and hard shaft deeper into my mouth. Wetting my lips more, I moved up...and then down....up...and down on you. I liked going slow at first, so you could feel everything inch by inch.

I remember you muttering, "Oh my god, babyyyy..."

I loved hearing I was pleasing you. I went very, VERY slow, wanting our time together to be something we'd never forget.

I moaned, sucking you, expressing how enjoyable it was to have you in my mouth for the first time. You caressed your hands down my shoulders and arms, your breath hitching in your throat here and there as you tried to hold back from exploding into my warm, inviting mouth.

"Fuck...that feels so good..." is all you could breathlessly get out and I just hummed in agreement as I reached my palm to

twist slowly around the base of your cock while my tongue taunted your head and tip. I got you close, so you reached down to pull me up to your lips, kissing me deep and moaning into my mouth, tasting me after I'd sucked and tasted you.

You whispered, "Here, baby..." then stood up, turning me, and laying me down on the bed, opening my legs to see me before you. You were pleased with how I looked; you groaned as you opened my vulva and lips with your warm hands. I liked your gentle touch, so I let you have me.

You leaned down, driving your mouth and tongue into me. I remember gasping because you knew what you were doing. Waves of pleasure seared through me. I think it was at that moment, my soul had invited you in.

You knelt on the floor, your mouth fully sinking into me. You began using your tongue and lips to propel me into another world. Your world. I couldn't help but arch up towards you. Your oral play was something I'd felt I'd missed despite never having had you before. It was as if you knew my body already!

Your mouth continued its exploration, your tongue moving a bit faster, flicking as you kept in perfect time with my slow rocking hips and heightening arousal. I was impressed you knew exactly where to put your mouth and tongue; your commitment to my growing pleasure was obvious.

"Holy fuck..." is all I could muster as your hands traveled up to hold my hips, your mouth holding me down to the bed. I felt a familiar fire erupt within me, and my breathing began to hitch. I remember reaching up with one hand to cover my mouth while my other hand grasped at the comforter on the bed!

You started to pick up the pace and groaned, loving how I was responding. I could feel your smile and your desire to overwhelm me. I realized I couldn't take it any longer and stopped trying to control my body from doing what it wanted. What you wanted! I knew I was very orgasmic, and since you were wanting me to surrender, I allowed my body to succumb to your control. I whimpered beneath the hand over my mouth, my breathing becoming louder through my nose. You took that as a sign to increase your tongue movements and pressed in causing me to crash into my first explosive orgasm with you ever....

it
was
bliss...

I couldn't help but whimper, my hand flying off my mouth as I grabbed at your shoulder begging, "Gunnar!" Your name reverberated abruptly in the quiet of the room and you liked the sound of it coming from my lips, you said. You released from me and stood watching how you'd disarmed me.

"Beautiful..." was all you purred, running your fingertips along my breasts and tummy. Your gorgeous frame and adonis-like body stood hovering over me, and you looked as if you wanted to do everything all at once.

I tried to recover, wanting all of you, my breath returning slightly. I could tell you were staring at me, committing my orgasmic ways to memory.

I moved quicker than I thought I could and stood up, turning you to lie on your back on my tiny bed. I loved that you stretched out to your full length on it, not quite sure what was going to happen, but willing to trust me. Our oral introductions had gone satisfyingly well, so you seemed eager for what was next.

"Here. My turn." I smiled down at you and straddled over you.

"Okay..." was all you whispered, a smile pressed on your lips as you watched me climb up on top of you. "Oh myyyyyy..." came next, and you drew out the phrase, curious. I know you weren't expecting me to want to take you so soon, and on top, but you didn't complain.

I remember I slid my hands into yours and put them over your head near the rungs of the bed, my mouth coming down onto yours to taste me on your lips. I kissed you deeply, rocking my hips up and down to lubricate your shaft with my dripping slickness.

I then released from your lips and looked into your eyes in the dimly lit room asking, "Are you sure?"

"Yes." You answered quickly.

"Are you positive?" I said as I reached to the side of your head and whispered in your ear making sure the second sentence was clearly heard. "Once we do this, we can never go back." I explained. I wanted to make certain you were as sure as I was. Consent is important.

"I am..." is what you whispered to me as you pressed your large cock up into my moistness, showing me your answer and how much you wanted me. Both of us were being decidedly greedy and crossing a line as technically we were both still married to people we no longer wanted to be with. However, you sounded as if you were very certain and that made me even more so.

I reached up and closed your fingers around the rungs of my bed frame. I wanted you to hold onto the bed. I brought my arms down to the sides of your overly built chest and lifted my hips up so I could slide down on top of your fevered, erect penis.

I looked at you as I tried to open to you; you were very large, and your tip entered but reached my tightness and slowed. You opened your mouth to gasp. I slowly sunk down over you; you stretched me open and the bliss was something we both hadn't expected.

"Fuck..." I moved up and then sunk down deeper, my body finally relenting to your girth. The pleasure of your initial penetration was something neither of us would ever forget.

I was worried I would be a bit small for you, and although the very first entrance proved it true, we seemed not to notice over our unified gasps. I sunk slowly down fully on you, opening to you, letting my slickness surround you. Meanwhile, you were burrowing yourself into me, making sure we both felt we had come home. The pleasure was incredible...indescribable even.

I whimpered-a sound of surrender and relief that was music to your ears. You moaned and removed your hands from the bed to bring them down and cradle my hips, pulling me so you could sink deeper.

"Oh my god, you are so tight...your pussy is so tight, baby..."

You couldn't believe the feeling of me and wanted more and more as I glided so expertly farther down and squeezed you as you reached the apex of my cervix. It was as if my body was made just for you, and you could feel me deep inside suckling at the tip of your cock.

"Youuuuu...feel so damn good. Oh my god, I didn't think..." I lost my words at the sheer, unapologetic pleasure coursing all through my body. I hadn't felt a man like this...ever.

"Think?" You looked up at me, wanting me to finish my sentence.

"...didn't think...it would be like this...feel this...oh my god..." I couldn't explain myself. "First-time Sex" has never been this good." Admittedly, I hadn't been with a lot of men, but I'd never experienced such pleasure the first time with any other. You continued filling and stretching me so completely; the bliss came with each slow, sultry thrust.

"...uh...your..." You were lost in the movements of my body and hips.

I kissed your mouth then pushed my hands and lifted myself up to sit upright on you, your cock filling me even more and causing us both to lose ourselves in the pleasure. The thrilling sensation made me begin to rock my hips so that you moved a bit deeper, my hands finding my hair, my lungs opening for more air as my chest expanded revealing my full breasts above you.

You looked up at me. "Oh my yes..." You liked how I picked up the pace, trying to match your breath. Your warm, strong hands trailed up from my hips to my nipples. "Where... do you want me to..."

"Wherever you choose. I want you to cum where you want to." I brought my hands down and ran my palms down your chest, caressing your hard nipples. I smiled at you, giving you permission.

"I can cum inside you?" You searched my face, not quite sure of what I meant by where "you want to".

I smiled wider. "Of course." I taunted you by picking up my rhythm, wanting to make sure you understood my decision. Your eyebrows raised slightly, shocked at how I wanted you. I thought it odd that you would ask if you could cum inside me. I could sense you'd been instructed not to with someone, somewhere along in life, scolded maybe, or even shamed. Placing a hand on your chest and one on your thigh behind me, I picked up the pace as if you were my stallion to be tamed. You sucked air in through your teeth again and grabbed at my hips.

"Can we slow it down a little, baby? ...I don't...I want to hold back..." You let me know you were getting too close and gently pulled me to the side, laying me down on the bed beneath you.

I was impressed not only with your gorgeous body, but how swiftly you could maneuver yours...and mine... I opened to you, wanting to feel you closer. Missionary was a favorite position and I wanted to feel you deep in my pussy and on my amazingly, sensitive clit.

You wrapped your arms around me, and I responded by grabbing at your lats. Your mouth came crashing down on mine as your cock drove forward and as far as my body could allow. I moaned into your mouth; the ecstasy was more than I could handle. You removed your mouth from mine, driving into me again and wanting to hear me. You liked hearing my breathless whimpers.

You thrust again and I brought a hand to my mouth to cover the sounds I'd not made with any other man before. I felt as if you were taking over my entire body and there was nothing I could do, or wanted to do, to stop it. Your body was the perfect fit for me. Your weight crushed me in the most magnificent way.

I grabbed at your back again, then down to your muscular tush, pulling you in, wanting you deeper and deeper despite how your large size was stretching me. You moved your lips to meet mine again, your thrusts pushing me closer to another blissful orgasm.

"Oh babyyyy..." You purred. "You...are...soooo..."

I was nearing my climax. You sensed it and pulled out of me, sliding down my body to finish me again with your mouth! I was confused but arched instinctively towards your hungry lips. You wanted to taste me again as I came, and you, told me so as you moved to slide your tongue in me, around me, and even into my ass.

I gasped. I didn't know what to feel as every part of my body was tingling. Then you moved your tongue up to my clit again and began flicking and sucking it faster and faster, I arched up and unexpectedly crashed over into another glorious orgasm! I wanted to cry your name again but instead covered my mouth. My body pulsed and convulsed and almost bucked. I fell into exhausted bliss, and you stood up and took a step back to look down at my soaked and swollen pussy.

"Oh my god, you are beautiful..." You couldn't seem to believe how sexual I was. Everything texted between us was slowly coming to fruition. "You have no idea how amazing you look in the lighting in here...and spread open before me..."

Your strong fingers gently slid into my slickness, my softness gripping you as if wanting more. You watched, letting me catch my breath, then took my hand standing me up, my legs shaking.

You walked me over to my long white chaise lounge chair and laid me down on it with my legs open. You climbed over me and slid into me slick and easy. You thrust deep, making me gasp at the pressure of your large cock in me. You continued over and over, teasing and tantalizing me until my breath labored.

You then stood up, again pulling me upright, with my hand. I followed, struggling to walk, my legs still weak from cumming and your glorious weight pressing on the length of my body. When we reached the bed, I took control, pushing you down. Your hands came up wanting to pull me over you, but instead, I wrapped my mouth around your cock and took you deep into my throat. I loved the taste of us together.

"Ohhhhh baby...the...way you..."

"Mmmmmm..." I moaned, sucking you slow as I moved up and down your shaft. You have a magnificent dick, and I made sure to show you just how much I liked it.

You lifted your head to watch me in the romantic glow of the room. You moved my hair to the side. "That feels...so good... do you like the taste of us?"

I smiled and nodded.

"Would you want to swallow me?" Your head lowered and then lifted again to see my answer.

"Mm hmmm...." I agreed, my mouth and lips moving along your length then to your tip. I swirled my tongue around in circles to make sure you understood my agreement.

Your head hit the pillow again. "Oh, my god...I've never been..." Your words halted and you brought your hands down to me and pulled me up to you wanting to kiss me deeply. You were getting close in my mouth but stopped me before I could bring you to the edge.

You moaned into my mouth, kissing me again and again, tasting me mixed with your precum. You thought I was breathtaking. Never had you had a woman like me before.

I tried to catch my breath, realizing that I'd had two orgasms and you still hadn't had one...you were still holding off. I was impressed with your control.

I stood up turning you on the bed and positioning you lengthwise again, with your head on my pillow. Since you almost came when I was on top of you before, I wanted to ride you again. I thought about straddling you in reverse-cowgirl but realized we hadn't talked of it yet and it might be too impersonal to be facing away from you as you came for the first time ever with me. I decided to bring that up another time and instead faced you again, looking down at your face full of want and desire for me.

You reached for me. It'd been so long since someone wanted me...even saw me naked. You seemed to really want to, and I liked that. I decided I was going to give you a ride you'd never forget.

I sunk down over you, your girth making my breath rush through my teeth. I started my deep, sultry hip rocking and your chest muscles bulged as you gripped my hips. One of your hands slid slowly up my stomach to my breast. You squeezed it just enough to send surges of pleasure through me. I picked up my pace, then, causing your breathing to quicken as you tried to mutter something, but you were beyond the point of forming a coherent sentence. I moved even faster trying to match your breath, then humped you deeper, squeezing you inside me faster, and faster, and faster...

The room fell silent. You clenched your whole body as you gripped onto my hips with force. You began to pump and pulse inside me. I looked down at you, silent, serene-looking, and I experienced elation as I felt you pump and spill your cum inside me. You looked so hot, finally letting go, as if it'd been years since you allowed yourself to feel such bliss. It pleased me to be able to pleasure you so much. You smiled, you brought one hand up to hold your forehead, and then let your arm fall to the pillow.

"Are...you okay?" I whispered placing a hand on your heart. It concerned me slightly that you'd internalized your orgasm and went quiet, holding your breath. You had a look that. Appeared to be a mixture of disbelief and satisfaction.

You nodded. "Just...numb...my face and feet...numb..." You smiled wider and released a chuckle.

I started to get off of you and to give you some space, but you moved to your side and pulled me to you, my ass up against your crotch. You wrapped a strong arm around me and I liked how safe it felt, your breath on my neck, the warmth of you cradling my back. You were still hard, surprisingly, and not getting soft.

You pushed your cock, slick and dripping, between my tush and thighs, then pushed your tip inside my vulva, pulling me to you.

"You've still got me hard," You whispered softly into my ear.

I moaned. "Mmmmm....yes, how nice...." I liked how you were sliding slowly in and then out again, then a little farther, parting my opening, then out again, tantalizing and taunting me towards more pleasure. I arched back towards you, and you took the opportunity to slide your mouth to my neck while pressing more and entering me from behind. My eyes rolled back, and intense pleasure moved up and down my spine as your girth parted me and your mouth suckled at my neck, sending shivering pleasure down my body. I couldn't believe you were still so aroused after your climax.

My mind started to drift back into the transcendence of my Ayahuasca ceremony and I fought between wanting the high of the plant medicine and the high of you.

Your lips sucked again at my neck, biting gently and bringing me back to the room. I reached a hand up and behind to find your neck, caressing your muscles and pulling you in. The pleasure you were granting me left me speechless and sucking air into my lungs to stay conscious. I felt as if I would float away if I weren't grounded by your cradling arm and hard cock inside me from behind...thrusting and thrusting.

"Feel how you keep me hard, baby? Feel me deep inside you?"

I nodded, unable to find words, never wanting you to stop. Your hand slid up to my breast as you sunk your mouth down into my neck again and pushed your cock even deeper. I arched back, meeting you, wanting you, my hand moving to clasp your hand to my breast. A loud moan escaped me, and I tried to remember to be quiet. You were making it difficult, your multiple stimulations driving me mad. Your pelvic play inviting me to grip and squeeze around you.

Your mouth released, "You...are sooooo..." Suddenly, you stopped. "Here, I want to feel you baby...I want to cum in you again..."

You moved down the bed and up onto your knees pulling my hips towards you, so that I was on all fours. I couldn't believe how quickly you moved; your energy appeared to be endless.

"Is it okay to, baby?" You whispered, entering me with your thick, hot penetration from behind.

I moaned, trying to respond. "Yes, of course... mmmmm..."

I pushed back to you, letting you fill me deeper from behind, and exhaled, a moan escaping me at the heightened sensation of the sheer size of you inside me, doggie style. I arched down, my tush high, pushing back, meeting you, enjoying the feeling of your balls caressing my clit. You felt amazing and I wanted you deeper and deeper.

You drove into me, your own exhales matching mine.

"Oh my...babyyyyy."

You thrust again, and again, over and over as I pushed back to meet you and squeeze you inside my womb. You started to move faster, your strong hands gripping my hips, one hand moving to run down along my spine. I arched upwards, your tender touch arousing me. I moved faster and faster, hearing you getting closer, ready to cum again so soon. Suddenly you froze, your seed pumping into me. I kept my hips moving and made circular motions surrounding you with my dripping womb, feeling you pulse and pump inside me. The ecstasy was like no other I had experienced before...

***

Peg's eyes opened one last time. She smiled in the dark, the memories making her feel full in her heart but causing a deep yearning in her body. She'd loved him even from that first time. She turned to her side and inhaled deep. Her eyes closed slowly as visions of him returned while her body drifted off to sleep...*finally.*

Chapter 10
ORDERLY

Dereck pulled out of Janson Argyle's ass and came all over his low back, his cum white against dark skin. Janson cooed and looked back over his shoulder biting his knuckle. He liked the new, twisted fat psych patient and his bi-sexual tendencies, despite his smaller cock size. He was a perfect size for anal but he really wasn't sure how he could please a woman.

He did find it weird that he moaned and chanted the name **Peg** when he was fucking him. He'd heard that, that was the name of his ex who he'd actually shot and kidnapped, which was why he was in Desert View Psychiatric Hospital.

Janson knew he should report the behavior but it'd been a long time since he'd had a boyfriend. He didn't want to ruin it.

"Wow, big boy, you were a bit more savage tonight."

Dereck looked down at Janson's hairy ass and felt disgust. He missed Peg's smooth, tight, tanned skin. He detested fucking Janson when Gunnar O'Clery was six hours away with Peg. Part of him wanted to reach down and choke the life out of the scrawny orderly. He didn't have it in him. Even though he was in a unit with crazy murderers and psychotic criminals, he just wasn't able to bring himself to kill...*yet*.

"You can get the fuck out now. I'm tired."

Dereck stepped back, pulled his pants up, and turned to walk towards the door to go wash his dick.

Janson lowered his tone, pissed to be treated like used trash again because Dereck had fragile masculinity, "Where do you think you're going?"

"To shower your shit off my dick."

"Oh no no no, sweets. The unit is down for the evening. No showering. And with that attitude you can sleep with my flavor on you all night."

Janson stood up and took a package of wet wipes out of his scrubs pocket, pulled one out and reached around to clean his back off staring at Dereck, a smirk forming at the corners of his mouth.

Dereck looked at the almost-full pack. "I'm sorry. Can I please have a few of those?"

He could see the keys hanging from Janson's pants and knew he could easily let him into the showers but with the way he's treated him that wasn't going to happen.

"And why would I give you anything now?"

"I apologize. I'm just having a hard time-"

"Oh honey, you don't have to tell me. You wreak of bi-polar abuse, especially after you spill your load in or on me. You're going to have to work on that if you want to keep doing this. Once or twice is understandable but, every damn time? You must be out ya mind, *chubbers* if you think you can treat me like a cum-dumpster."

Janson aggressively took another wipe and bend over to clean his own ass, letting Dereck watch him.

"Again, I apologize. You're right. I need to treat you better."

"Mmm hmmm."

"I'll let you clean it."

Dereck looked at Janson with his piercing black eyes and backed up, pulling his pants down, then sitting on the bed opening his legs.

Janson smiled, warming to him, "Okay, but only if you tell me who Peg is while I do so."

Dereck was annoyed but didn't dare show it as he could see he was winning at manipulating the little pansy.

"Peg? Yeah, okay. What do you want to know?"

Janson walked over and knelt down in front of him, "Well, for starters, why is it you can only cum if you say her name? She's not your mom or something, is she?"

Dereck felt a rage well up from the pit of his stomach and, before he knew, it he reached out placing his palms on either side of Janson's head. He torqued his hands in opposite directions with a force he hadn't felt since Desert Storm...snapping Janson's neck in one swift move. He let go and watched his limp body fall to the floor. He was dead. His entire life over in one...rapid motion.

Dereck laid his head back on the bed and stared at the ceiling, a smile creeping along his lips. The voice in his head had returned. ***There you are, we've been waiting for you...welcome back.***

Peg climbed under the covers and exhaled as her body sunk into the mattress. She ached in areas of her body she didn't even realize she used just to get through the day. She knew it was her damn C-PTSD and the overthinking of everything lately. Trying to get back into life and living without him was proving to be overly exhausting.

Laying on her back she craned a leg open and ran her hand down her silk pajama bottoms and over her vulva. She liked how it felt like his warm hand, his strong yet gentle touch. She loved how tough he could be, how intense, yet not once did he ever touch her with force or cause her pain. He was so incredibly intense and yet so vulnerable with her. She loved the contrast and how they fit so perfectly into each other's arms...and bodies.

She took the pad of her index finger and began to circle her clit slowly, thinking of him and how his mouth and tongue would drive her wild. Inside she could almost feel his engorged cock penetrating and thrusting all the way to her cervix. A surge of pleasure rang through her body. She felt so much desire for him in her mind that her body was responding as if he were there.

Her mind wandered as her fingers gently played. She thought of the time when Gunnar had asked her if she would leave her door unlocked so he could come in as she was pleasing herself with her toy. Peg would never have done that for Dereck; she'd never have felt comfortable enough nor wanted to please him in that way. But with Gunnar, she'd wanted to give him the world, and the way he'd treated her and her body had given her the confidence to do most almost anything.

She'd put on heels and lingerie for him and when he'd walked in, she'd had her panties pulled to the side and the little handheld vibrator he'd bought her sliding up and down along her clit hood, causing waves of pleasure for him to see.

His eyes dilated and fixed on her sensual movements. Then he'd lifted them to meet her gaze. She'd sent him a sultry look before her breathing had become labored as she saw his plump muscles rippled beneath his clothing.

He'd locked the door, thrown his gun and hat to the couch, and made his way to her. She had been a sight to behold beneath his touch as he'd slid two fingers inside of her and kissed her sweetly to connect their energy.

Peg reached for him and found he was already hard beneath his gym pants. His mouth slid down an to her neck, his lips opening to allow his tongue and mouth to suck hard, marking her where her hair would cover it. She'd arched up and exhaled trying to suppress her want but not able to beneath his fevered mouth.

All the things they had done that day began to run through her mind. His mouth had moved down and onto her clit as his fingers gently continued to explore inside of her. She'd pulled at his shirt, wanting him naked. He'd obliged and removed his clothing while gazing deep into her eyes, his hunger apparent. He'd leaned in again, doing all that he knew made her surrender to him, preparing her for the next three hours of blissful connection... *their* connection.

G unnar looked over, annoyed at everyone in the room. They were all staring at the monitor, observing the multiple fuck-ups, one after another as the shootout unfolded on the screen with little discipline, obvious disregard for life, and little recall of extensive training.

He sighed, unfolding his arms. He leaned forward, grabbing this keys and phone, and turned to look at the six FBI agents he was assigned to work with.

"This is not how things are done, guys. Not even our sheriff's department fucks up like this. Clean it up. Tomorrow, 0630, be here ready to follow my strategy as I had instructed. You got a problem with that, contact my higher ranks."

Gunnar stormed out dialing his boss's number though he wished he was calling Peg instead. He needed her so bad. He placed the phone to his ear and walked towards his truck. He felt the intensity of how dark his life had gotten. It was as if the light was going out.

Chapter 11

BREAKDOWN

P eg woke, feeling tears building. She didn't know why or what was going on that made her feel such sorrow, she just knew something was happening. He wasn't there to talk to, to text with, he was just...*gone*. She wanted to breakdown but she refused. She turned and reached for her cell:

Peg's Cell:
Hello Josephine?

Josephine's Cell:
Yes? Good morning.

I think...I need help

Missing him sweetie?

I'm not doing well.

Can you meet for breakfast?

Please?

How about Val's Diner in a half hour?

Thank you yes, I'll be there.

I'm glad you reached out.

***

Josephine watched Peg get out of her truck and walk briskly towards the entrance to the diner. She thought she looked beautiful in her cream-colored valor sweatsuit and matching Uggs. Peg was stunning, but in a way where she didn't seem to fuss or notice. She was the kind of woman that took care of herself then forgot about it after she left the house, focusing on other things. She wasn't overly insecure and constantly checking on her looks. It made her all the more alluring.

She slid into the booth across from Josephine and tried to smile, although her eyes were sad. She could tell Peg was trying to be strong.

"Okay. Tell me what happened to bring this on. It helps me to know in case there is a trigger."

Peg shook her head slowly, "That's the thing. Nothing. I was asleep and suddenly my eyes opened and a flood of...well, everything just bombarded me. I'm trying to process it."

She took a sip of the coffee Josephine ordered for her, although she never really touched the stuff.

Josephine reached to her and touched her hand. "Peg, you know you've been through hell, right? You were shot, kidnapped, underwent surgery, and left by the man who saved you from more than just your ex."

Peg raised her eyes, which were filling with tears she was trying to hold back.

"You have PTSD, darling, and it's going to affect you when it wants to, not when you think it should."

"That's the thing, Jo, I thought I was-"

"You are doing well. This is just part of it. Now, let me have it. Just start talking until you can't anymore and I'll do my job. Can you let me do my job?" She smiled and Peg nodded.

She leaned back against the booth, pushing her hair back as if she was readying herself for something physical, "I think I seek out and give attention to those I cannot obtain love from. I feel this is because of my childhood wounding. I want to be chosen so badly. Like, somehow, I feel it will prove I am lovable when actually I've always been lovable...I just need to remember that and believe it. I feel I have a chemical addiction...*to Gunnar*.

"I fought so hard to get away from my ex but, in the transition, I crossed paths with Gunnar and now I feel a pull towards him. He's left, and I don't know why, and it's killing me like I'm trying to get off heroin or some sort of drug. I feel like it's a chemical cocktail in my body. Like norepinephrine, adrenaline, and cortisol all released into my bloodstream...a stress response so to speak. When he'd come near me and touch me or make love to me, I felt ease and healing, like everything was going to be okay but, now that he's gone, I feel like I'm in withdrawal. I've been abandoned again. He said he loved me, but he left! I feel like I'm a fucking mess! Like I'm twisted and drawn to the UNLOVE I felt in childhood. I want to believe he loves me, but he left! Why do I love those who cannot prioritize me? He couldn't make me a priority...so he left! I don't understand, Jo. I don't fucking know what the fuck love is...and somehow...somehow I needed him to show me that my fucking journey is to find out what the fuck love really is..."

Jo smiled at Peg in the same way she smiled at her adult children when they discovered something profound while navigating parenthood. She was proud of Peg. Her confusion was an indication she was on the precipice of great knowledge about herself. She felt Peg was highly intelligent and had the drive and fight inside her to do the work of self awakening. She thought she an amazingly well-adjusted woman for all she'd been through.

"Why are you smiling, Jo?"

"You are lovely, Peg, just simply a beautiful soul."

Peg let a tear fall to her cheek, ignoring it. "What the fuck does that mean?"

"I know you feel vulnerable. I know this is hard but Peg, you are doing it."

"Doing what? Doing what, Jo?"

"Fighting. Fighting for the answers. Fighting to understand... fighting to love, to know love, and understand your struggle. I know now why he loves you."

Peg slapped her hand down. She looked out the window and smiled bitterly. "Great...well, could you tell me why? And why he's not fucking here?"

"He sacrificed Peg. He set you free...because he loves you. He's protecting you, Peg. I bet he's out there somewhere yearning and wishing he could be close to you but his love for you is bigger. He knows he can't put you first. He can't prioritize you the way you deserve. He doesn't want you to be last, like you were with Dereck...and until he can put you on the pedestal you deserve, he'll remove himself. He does love you Peg, he loves you more than you realize."

Peg brought her hands to her face to cover it. She sobbed quietly into them, letting herself finally break, mourning the love she could not get as a child from her mother, grieving that she went out and found a man just like her mother who'd abused her for twenty-some years, and yearning for the one man that had brought it all out of her and showed her by leaving that she must love herself, because she was worth it. No one on the outside could ever fulfill what was needed on the inside. She had to choose herself now. She had to forgive herself and work at loving herself in order to bring love in. Whether it be him or someone else. She wouldn't be able to have a real, healthy love until she chose herself. She...was...finally...breaking down...to break through. *Finally.*

G unnar returned to his apartment. Throwing his keys on the counter, he stormed straight to his room. He pulled his shirt over his head, throwing it to the floor and continuing on towards the shower. It had been a completely shitty day.

He pulled the covers up and slid into the king-sized bed half wet and fully naked. He lay on his back and stared up at the ceiling with his forearm across his forehead. Every part of him wanted to get in the truck and drive to her, take her in his arms and never let her go. He could sense her, feel her breath on his skin, how her voice sounded in the quiet of her room as he pleasured every inch of her body. He missed how she would remind him of how desirable he was, how she loved his body...

Gunnar began to drift off. Visions of her swam through his mind. He remembered the time she was out with her friend at a local bar just talking and she'd left because he wanted to see her after a day resting in bed and yearning for her. He'd tried to stay away, even did four shots of fireball, but nothing had helped ease the desire he had for her.

It had been late, about ten-thirty, when he'd suddenly found himself walking beside her from her truck to her door. She'd been wearing heels, dress shorts, and a black sleeveless shirt. He'd reached down as she'd unlocked the house, where her roommates were sleeping, and ran his middle finger along the cleft of her ass cheek. His dick hitched as he'd felt the smoothness of her freshly shaven body, knowing he'd be inside her tight womb in a matter of minutes.

He remembered how quiet they'd been on their way to her room. He'd locked the door and searched for her in the dark until she could turn on the nightlight. The glow of her physique in the dim light reminded him of their first time.

Gunnar hadn't thought about clothes, or work, or stress, or anything. He'd pushed her down on the bed, his body coming down on hers, his mouth and tongue exploring the taste of faint whiskey on her breath. He'd pressed his hips forward, his hard cock tantalizing her clit beneath her thin clothing, making her moan into his mouth the way he liked. Peg loved how he'd moved into and onto her. She rewarded him by wrapping her arms and legs around him, drawing him in. He'd felt as if everything in the world just disappeared when Peg embraced him.

He remembered how he'd savagely fucked her that night. She'd welcomed every hard thrust, every deep slam into her. She'd moved with him like a wave and had sensed how much he'd needed her then...as he needed her now.

Anger flowed through him. He was mad at how things had gone after he left the hospital. How his ex had threatened him. How he'd had to leave to get away but also to protect Peg. He hated that he'd left her with no explanation. He hated all of this...and himself for not loving her the way she needed. *The way she deserved.*

***

Peg's Journal Entry:

Today...was rough! I've been trying so hard to hold it together, but I miss him so much. My heart aches terribly. I've been trying to distract myself and found myself thinking of the first time we did anal. I'd promised him that we would try it and, when I got more and more comfortable with him, I was able to trust him enough to suggest it.

*After an hour of doing all our favorite things and both cumming a couple of times, I mentioned to him that I'd like to try it. I told him I would be honored to be his **first** experience.*

He asked if I was sure, and I could tell he wanted it so bad as his face was like a curious little boy. I taught him about lube, and he was so respectful and gentle with it. It was a warming lube, so it felt amazing for both of us.

I told him since he was "sized" it may take me a bit to relax and allow my body to accept him. He listened and only pressed into me when I was ready and instructed him to. We were on our sides, which I explained was preferable for me as "things" were more relaxed.

To my surprise my body wanted him so much that he moved in easily, after three or four sloooooooow presses. He felt fucking phenomenal after my body eased around him. He used small, slow thrusts and I was able to press back against him, allowing him, deeper and deeper. His arms around me, his body pleasuring mine, his breath in my hair...his voice murmuring my name..."Oh, Peg...oh my...."

It was super slow and felt magical. I enjoyed him more than anyone before and honestly moved to a new level of trust with him. I could tell his mind was blown and when he came with me...he came loooong which left him quiet with satiated. It felt wonderful to find that level of pleasure with him. There wasn't anything I couldn't enjoy with him. God...I miss him.

Chapter 12
CHEATERS

Josephine's Cell:
Got a minute?

Aileen's Cell:
Always, you ok?

I am but our girl isn't. Feel so bad for Peg.

She's really going through it huh?

So strong yet...not.

Those are the best kind

True. Her heart is broken. He just left and she has no closure.

You need me to find him Jo? I really didn't want to get involved again.

I don't know. I just hate to see her so busted up you know?

I haven't checked in on her in a while. I'm going to give her a call.

That would be nice. No hitting on her A.

I don't you lil' shit.

Lol, k.

I'll call her here in a few.

You could meet her out, get yourself out of that house.

Fuck that, it's too peopleeeeee out.

Lordy

I'll invite her over okay?

Whatevs

You cranky or something?

No, just feel sad for the woman. All the shit her ex put her through...Gunnar made it better by loving on her, then she gets shot, kidnapped, and rescued by him only to be abandoned after being told she was loved.

That's men for ya

No, something seems off

He may have gone back to his wife Jo

True

They do that. I can find out in probably two seconds.

It doesn't matter, she'd still have to repair herself

Repair?

Heal, you know what I meant smartass.

Lol...you need to get laid

Kettle...black...ummmmmm

84

Ha! Good idea. I'll call Peg now.

Don't even think of it carpet-licker

That made me laugh hard

How would you know what hard even is...

Wow, feisty...stop, you're giving me wood

Jeeeeeeezus christ Aileen, you are the most fucked up human I know I swear.

And don't you forget it!

Later-

Lol

***

Aileen dialed Peg's number and waited.

"Peg Law." She answered in a soft voice.

"Hello Ms. Law. How are you?"

"Aileen?"

"Yep, wondering how you're holding up?"

"I was just asking Jo about you last night."

Aileen knew that was true. "Still kicking, honey. Listen, I haven't talked to you in weeks, got any time for an old gal?"

"Of course. What were you thinking?"

"Well, I don't go out much, but I'd love some company here at my home. Feel like sharing a bottle of wine and catching up?"

Peg smiled on the other end. "That sounds great."

"Can you make it tonight after you close up?"

"Yes, I close at six today. Can I bring something?"

Aileen thought for a moment. "I do love a nice charcuterie board."

"Me too. You got it."

"See you at six thirty."

"See you then."

***

Richie closed the front door behind him and walked across the yard towards the front door of Peg's house. Her truck wasn't parked out front, but he was hoping to find out where she was from one of her roommates. He figured it was worth a shot and he had not met them yet. He pushed the button on the ring camera and waited.

"Yes?" A rough female voice came through; Richie was certain it wasn't Peg's.

"Uh, hi, is Peg around?"

"Who's asking?" Rena was not feeling warm.

"Hi I'm Richie Holmes, your new neighbor next door."

"Oh, the one with all the Audis parked all over?"

"Uhhhh, yep that would be me."

Rena was letting him know about her disapproval in her passive aggressive way. "Yeah, well Peg should be home any minute, you got a message?"

Richie smiled realizing how aggressive Peg's roommates must feel after she was almost murdered in their doorway by Dereck. The guy just destroyed everything he was near.

"Oh, nothing urgent, just have a question for her. I'll catch her another time."

"Yep."

86

"Well, thank you."

"Yep."

Richie turned, shaking his head as he walked back towards his house. He'd wanted to invite Peg, and possibly her roommates, over for dinner but had changed his mind. From his brie encounter with Rena, he understood that no introductions would be made, no names given, and no one was coming to the door for a greeting. He huffed a small laugh realizing Peg, despite having been harmed, was probably the friendliest person on her street.

***

Aileen watched Peg move silently around and take a seat on the same barstool Gunnar had when he was sitting at her counter months prior. She was stunning. She could see why he desired her. She had beautiful blonde hair, and her bone structure was exquisite. She had a pleasing face-the kind that made you feel you were always making her happy.

"I'm so glad you could make it over. We haven't talked enough."

Peg nodded. "True. I appreciated you checking in on me while I was in the hospital and after I returned home. Thank you.'

Aileen stood across the counter and reached for a piece of cheese as Peg unwrapped the snacks. She poured them both a full glass of wine.

"Of course. How are you feeling now? It seems you're fully recovered by the way you're moving."

"I'm doing better than the doctors expected. I think it may be from all the gym time prior. I honestly couldn't wait to get back to my workouts."

Aileen smiled. "I bet. You've been okay with getting out and keeping your practice open?"

"I have, yes. Knowing that Dereck is no longer around helps. I don't know how I'd handle it if he were still in the same town."

"Yes. We all feel safer now that Gunnar took care of him."

Peg sipped her wine and nodded, unable to answer. Aileen could see the pain in her as her eyes moved to the artworks on the walls, as if looking for distraction.

I'm sorry Peg, I just rattled on without-"

"No, that's quite alright. You have a point. Life is easier now with what Gunnar did."

"Let's discuss it. Come on, my couches are much more comfortable."

Aileen picked up her wine and the charcuterie board and walked into the living room. Peg followed suit.

"Your home is beautiful." She recognized her home was only seven houses down the street from her own home she once shared with Dereck. She knew at some point she was going to have to visit it and see all that Dereck had ruined of the life they'd built.

Aileen knew she was being kind, "Thank you. Here, sit here so you can put your glass on the table."

"Thank you."

"I'm just going to come out and ask honey, do you feel Gunnar left you or that he's away on work?"

"I don't know, Aileen. I'd hope no matter what he would send me a note, or something."

"Not even a text, huh?"

"No. No response to mine either."

"Just left?"

"I think at the end of the day I just hope he's happy and at peace."

"That's love, darling."

Peg sipped her wine, unable to answer.

Aileen sat across from her making eye contact. "What's the worst that could happen Peg?"

"Death? Him returning to his ex...or wife, or whatever the situation was?"

"Why?"

"I guess because then I'd have to believe he didn't love me the way he'd said."

Aileen softened. "A man can love you to death Peg and even if he returns to his wife. You're lovable in all scenarios."

Peg smiled. "You're kind."

"Peg, I'm not trying to be kind. I'm telling you what I know of studying human behavior for years of my career."

"Yeah."

"I can tell you're hurting. Not only did you survive the trauma of your ex and all his manipulation you're now left with wondering if the love of your life manipulated you too, right?"

"It's taking all my strength to just keep going."

"You're doing it. You are one of the strongest women Jo and I know, girl."

Peg was aware that they both talked about her, but they'd been a source of friendship, so she didn't mind.

"I'm trying. Some days are just so empty without him."

"Sometimes it's easier to feel anger...because it creates some sort of connection."

"I don't want to be angry at him."

"I know sweetie. So do you feel he cheated then?"

"What do you mean?"

"Do you feel he just used you...and went back to his shitty marriage? Like, just cheated for awhile and went back to what was familiar?"

Peg shrugged. The thought had crossed her mind and was the source of her anger.

"Let's discuss cheating, shall we?"

"Do we have to? I was married to a cheater. I think I've had my fill."

Aileen smiled knowing this was how she could help Peg, "Exactly. Let's start there. Your ex was a cheater from the get-go right?"

"From what I learned later, yes. He cheated from the beginning."

"Okay, so we know there are five reasons why someone cheats. You've studied this in your relationship coaching, right?"

Peg nodded.

"So, we have the INSECURE CHEATERS:

- they struggle with self-esteem
- they feel powerless, uneducated, and aged
- they seek validation through the cheating act
- they use the "spark of interest" to feel desired, wanted, and worthy

INTENSE EMOTIONAL CHEATERS:

- they feel their relationship has fallen into a boring comfort zone
- they want to FEEL something
- they seek intensity through the cheating act
- they desire a newly formed relationship even if the old one is fine

INHERENT SELFISH CHEATERS:
- they feel they DESERVE more even if they love their partner
- they feel vows are something to be worked around
- they don't sacrifice for their relationship
- They feel the "grass is greener" affect

"LIFE NOT LIVED" CHEATERS:
- they yearn for "the life that could have been" if they'd had more experiences
- they feel there is a lover that "got away"
- they feel there is a lover that "never was"
- they are overly curious
- They yearn for a different pathway than what they were groomed in

TRANSGRESSION CHEATER:
- they struggle with the "child stealing a cookie" thought
- they feel forbidden-ness is extra desirable
- they seek cheating because it's seen as wrong and they need to feel "special" and "desired"
- they see getting away with it as attractive, a win

Peg nodded. She remembered all of it.
"Well, you've just described my ex to a T."
Aileen leaned back. "And Gunnar?"
"It's everything I hope he isn't."
"What would make him none of these cheaters?"
Peg shrugged, her eyes welling up with tears.
"Choosing you, right?"
"Fuck if I know, Aileen."

"What if he did choose you Peg? What if no matter where in the world he is, his heart beats for only you?"

Peg put her wine down and buried her face in her hands. She'd done this the night previous with Josephine. She was so exhausted with thinking about it all, with hoping, with needing to know.

"I'm not trying to hurt you more, Peg."

Peg looked up. The pain in her eyes was almost unbearable for Aileen to see. She suddenly started to regret bringing up such heavy conversation.

"No, I know that you're trying to help me logic through this, Aileen. I know your heart is in the right place. I'm just not there yet. I'd like to be able to decide on this. I need to be able to work through why he said he loved me...then left. Why he saved me... then fucking broke me..."

Aileen leaned forward and looked her in they eyes. "Peg, perhaps he's just simply being...well, a man who doesn't know... *yet*."

"Yet?"

"Yeah...yet."

Chapter 13

MISERABLE

Dereck reached down into Janson Argyle's scrub side pocket and took a set of keys he'd watched him use for all the doors in the ward. They would help but what he really needed were the keys to Janson's stupid fucking minivan that he'd watched him speed into the parking lot in when he was late for his shift.

He'd specifically targeted Janson because he too was once a bisexual married husband with a minivan and kids. A total shit-show of unhappiness. The guy was almost too easy to manipulate and snapping his neck had been was even easier. Dereck didn't even care that he'd taken away the only source of income that Janson's wife and five kids had. He figured he'd helped Janson out of his miserable existence and if his wife and kids had to suffer, so be it. He suffered every day.

Reaching into Janson's other pockets, he found the set of personal keys and recognized the Ford Windstar key. He smiled, stepped over Janson's limp, dead body, and walked toward the door with the intent to make his ex-wife suffer next-for a second-and then provide her with a miserable death. This time he would not hesitate to end her life...or to end Gunnar's. He decided he would wipe them both from the face of the earth...but in bed... after he'd witnessed them fucking.

Richie hung up the phone confused. He'd never not been able to get a hold of Dereck when he called. The staff said they'd find him and have him call back. He didn't mind so much as the guy was not his favorite human.

He heard music coming from outside, a nice classic CCR song that never got old for him. He leaned to look out the window and saw Peg parking behind his white Audi. Jumping up, he moved swiftly towards the door. He was excited to finally see her again.

Peg came around the back of her truck to the passenger side and saw him approaching.

"Hey there!"

She tried to smile. "Hello Richie. How are you?"

He had a hopeful, excited look to him. "I'm well, how are you holding up Peg?"

"I'm alive."

"I'm glad. Hey I'd like to invite you over for steaks on the grill if I could. Are you free in about an hour?"

Peg wasn't entirely in the mood to try to be cordial but being alone sounded worse. She answered before she could talk herself out of it.

"I am, yes. Steaks sound great. Can I bring beer, a side, or... anything?"

"Nope. Got it all, just bring yourself. Oh, and comfy clothes are a must as I'm still unpacking and my house is uber casual."

She smiled. "Uber casual?"

"Okay, it's a shit-show but actually but I was trying to be cool. My son would have been proud of me for even using the word 'uber'."

"That's amusing."

"Glad I could make you smile."

"Be sure to tell him you inserted the word 'uber' into a complete sentence. I'll be sure to wear something comfortable, as I've about had it with these scrubs for the day."

"They look comfortable." He loved the way she paired a curvy scrub top over leggings. She was the hottest massage therapist he'd ever seen, and he wondered how she fit all her muscle under her uniform.

She looked down at her attire as if she'd not noticed it lately. "Oh yeah, well, they are but sometimes it's nice to not have to wear spandex."

"Oh, I see."

"Okay, so about an hour?"

"Yes, I'm going to go fire up the grill. I could use the company while cooking, so feel free to join me on the back porch whenever you're ready."

She smiled, hoping he was not thinking it was a date. "And... you're sure you don't need anything? Dessert, maybe?"

"I've got that too-if you're fine with ice cream sandwiches?"

"Love'em. Okay."

Richie started to back away clapping his hands then pointing at her, "Okay, see you in a bit."

Peg loaded her hands with sheets from the front of her truck and kicked the door shut with her foot. Smiling she said, "See you in a bit."

Dereck accelerated in the minivan annoyed at how the vehicle triggered him. Ice couldn't help recalling how defeated he had felt father had bought him a similar version of the stupid vehicle, years prior. His father had always stifled him.

As he merged onto the highway, he inhaled with relief. He'd gotten away with murder and now he was free to drive six hours back to Peg and get away with her murder too.

He wiped his brow, feeling the cold sweat on his hand. He wiped his palm along the drab gray scrub bottoms to dry it.

A laugh erupted from deep within his evil soul. He was free again and it had been easier to escape than he could have dreamed. Driving in the far-left lane, he turned on cruise control and eased back into the seat hoping the effects of the drugs would start to wear off soon. He was happy they'd been wearing off, although the voices were getting louder. He didn't mind, he was hoping they'd help him find Josephine Adeyo, Gunnar O'Clery, Peg, and eventually Richie Holmes-not necessarily in that order.

His eyes lowered as a red button lit up on the dash. The fuel needle was on E.

"Fucking shit!"

Chapter 14

DON'T STOP

Peg lay down on her bed for a second to stretch her spine and reset her system before heading next door to Richie's house. Her heartbeat in her chest reminded her of so many times before when she'd laid on her back at Gunnar's request. Her mind wandered to the time it had been twelve days since she'd seen him and was feeling down. He came to her, entered her room asking her to remain on the bed. He moaned as he took a good look at her. She had dressed in a tight sports bra and leggings, ready to go to the gym. He'd walked to her, opening her knees, and hooking his arms under her legs to pull her to the edge of the bed so he could press his hard cock into her warmth. His eyes bore into hers, desire deep within his gaze.

"See what you do to me?"

Peg had smiled, nodding and reaching her hands up to run them along his broad chest, caressing his nipples the way he liked. He'd mimicked her motions and moved his hands along her chest, pulling the fabric of her sports bra down and freeing one breast so he could see her hardened nipple before sinking his mouth down onto it, causing her to arch up into him. She'd wrapped her arms around his neck, not wanting him to stop as surges of pleasure rippled down through her body to her throbbing wetness. Gunnar could ignite all her senses with a mere flick of his tongue.

Realizing she was already drenched for him, he'd moved his hands to her ass and waist, grabbing at her clothing and pulling it off. Throwing her pants to the floor, he'd lunged forward, his hands opening her thighs and his mouth sinking down onto her vulva. He'd been hungry for her, but he'd known to remain gentle as he stimulated her most sensitive area.

Peg breathed heavily, and he'd ben lost for a moment in how much he adored her, loving that he could make her so beautifully vulnerable and that she wanted to give herself to him. He'd missed her but, instead of telling her, he was going to show her how much.

Standing up, he'd quickly stripped off his clothing before pulling her thighs to him and plunging into her wet, wanting pussy. He'd let out an exhale as she gasped. He'd pulled out almost all the way then slammed into her, knowing it would drive her wild. Sure enough, Peg cried out in pleasure, and he'd felt he owned her once again.

"Whose pussy is this baby? Whose beautiful body is this?"

Peg had opened her eyes, clawing at his chest, not wanting him to stop the incredible ecstasy.

"Yours...oh my god...all yours, baby."

Her face had contorted as he'd picked up the pace, fucking her a bit deeper and faster as she was nearing climax. He'd absolutely loved seeing her cum and he would have stopped at nothing to see her pleasured.

Peg's phone dinged with an incoming text message and her eyes opened.

"Shit!"

She sat up noticing her cell was on the floor and the light of it was illuminating the ceiling. She'd fallen asleep!

Gunnar stared out the window. His case was boring the shit out of him and leaving too much time to think. His thoughts wandered to Peg. He thought about how she was mostly tough, could handle much more than a woman should but there was also something soft and vulnerable he loved about her. Like him, he knew she needed comfort. He'd wanted to give her that, partly because of all the times he had longed. For it himself. There were so many times that he'd needed compassion, and understanding. And had failed to receive it. He knew he needed to give her that...still.

He remembered a time when he'd arrived in her room. He'd grabbed her and held her tight. He'd missed the feeling of her body against his. He had already been erect and throbbing for her as he'd walked up the driveway to her door. Peg had a power over his body he couldn't quite understand. Just the thought of her touch ignited him in ways he'd never felt before.

He hadn't said that he missed her, he hadn't been able to allow himself to do that, but his embrace had screamed it to her body. She had been vulnerable and shaking slightly. He'd wondered if her asshole ex had been harassing her and if she was just being tough about it. His lips had met hers and the feel of her warm, wet mouth had made his dick hitch beneath her hand that was already caressing him.

"See how hard you get me with just your kiss?" he'd whispered as she moved her soft velvet tongue to explore him.

She'd moaned and nodded. Suddenly, she'd slid down to her knees before him, freeing his cock from his clothing and engulfing him deep within her hot, moist mouth. Gunnar had breathed heavily, his head falling back. His body had tingled all over as her slow, sensual sucking created ecstasy throughout his body, down his shaft, and into his balls. No one had ever sucked his dick like Peg, making him feel so desired and wanted. She was a master at oral pleasure, and he'd felt honored each and every time she'd wanted to express her expertise. He'd felt as if he would explode.

"I want to be in you." He remembered pulling her shirt off and unfastening her bra.

"Mmmmmm...sir yes, sir...."

Peg had grabbed at the bottom of his shirt and pulled it over his head moving her mouth to his erect nipple. Gunnar moaned, placing his hand on her neck to pull her into him. He'd loved her mouth on him, her hands on his ribs, pressing around to his back, pulling him in.

Gunnar kissed her deeply, his tongue seeking her mouth, feeling the vibrations of her moans travel towards his heart. He'd tried so hard to not love her, but it hadn't worked.

He'd removed their clothing and climbed eagerly between her luscious thighs, his mouth coming down on hers, his cock sliding between her slick, wet folds, finding she was soaked with want for him. He'd pressed forward, her tight pussy slowly allowing him only so far.

Peg had released her mouth from his, needing space to breathe, as she accommodated his large size. Gunnar had slowed, allowing her to relax and sink around him. Both had moaned with satisfaction at the initial penetration. Their bodies had melded together in perfection, she'd moved towards him, he'd sunk deeper and deeper with each slow thrust.

"You...feel..." Gunnar's words caught in his throat.

"Yes...my...I'm..." She had wanted to tell him she was vibrating inside with want, shaking from his intense energy.

"-incredible...." He'd finished her sentence as he sunk deeper.

She'd muffled her exclamations of pleasure in the curve of his neck. He hadn't been able to believe how her wetness and snug velvety canal could feel so incredible every time they were together.

Peg had moved her mouth to his ear, "Can you feel how much you're wanted? How desired you are, baby? My body wants you like this all the time. Over...and over...and over...I never want this to stop."

Her hot breath in his ear had taunted him; her words had made him feel needed. She told him all that he'd wanted to hear. He'd nodded, thrusting slow and forward, unable to answer.

Gunnar had moved his hands from around her back and had taken each of her palms in his, pinning her hands to the bed, holding her down forcefully but with the tenderness he'd always showed. She'd exhaled and arched up farther to meet every thrust, every movement. Her body had ached and yearned each time he'd reached her limit, taunting and teasing with every inch of him inside her...rubbing his pelvis against her clit.

"Say it..." she'd whispered.

He'd pressed his mouth to her neck, suckling and sending shivers throughout her entire body that had settled in a tingling sensation at the tip of her clit. She'd gasped. He'd moved to the other side of her neck, waiting.

She'd breathlessly begged, "Say....my *name...*"

Gunnar had sunk down into her again, his mouth following, sending another electric ripple of pleasure through her that made her entire womb grip him tighter. He could feel her losing control.

"...*Peg...*" He'd done as requested and had released her hands to let her know she was free.

Peg had run her palms up his arms and to the sides of his face to hold his mouth to hers. She'd kissed him deep while thrusting her body up and around him, pulling him deeper into her with her legs.

Gunnar kissed her back and once she had his tongue in her mouth, as deep as he was in her pussy, she moved her hands down his strong back and to his ass, pulling him deeper into her.

Gunnar had been able to feel her desperate need for him, and it had made him begin to lose control. He'd withdrawn from her and stood up, pulling her towards the edge of the bed and turning her over onto her stomach.

Peg exhaled, realizing that he wanted her from behind. She'd shifted backwards toward his cock and arched to open to his penetration. He'd moved his hands along her lower back and around to her ass, pulling her hips to him.

"Oh...my...god...you have no idea how beautiful you are..." His whisper had echoed in the room. "Did you pleasure yourself today, baby?"

Peg had shaken her head. "No, I wanted you..."

Gunnar was pleased with her answer as he pushed in, deep and fast, filling her completely. Both had moaned at the same time. She'd grabbed the comforter beneath her; he'd gripped her waist tighter, careful not to hurt her. He'd never wanted to hurt her-she was a goddess to be worshiped.

"Jeeezus, you feel so...good..."

She had smiled, her face down against the soft bed that smelled of fresh laundry detergent and him.

"You are so good baby."

Gunnar had loved it when she'd said that and thrust a little more, feeling her move back towards him and grip him with her tight pussy.

"I...I dreamt of you...us...in the hot springs. The water reaching up to your ass, me entering you. The feel of you around me, the heat of you, the heat of the water..."

"Mmmmm...I like when you *dream*..."

Gunnar had felt his orgasm approaching. He'd pulled out of her and gently turned her over, diving into her vulva with his mouth, spreading her open sweetly with his hands. The movement had been so fluid and quick, Peg had had little time to adjust before her orgasm had begun to build. He'd moved his tongue faster, to match her breathing, and had been surprised at how quickly she'd begun to cry out and quiver beneath him! He'd loved to hear Peg's climax, nothing in the world sounded better than pleasing her!

He'd pulled away to let her breathe and regain her strength. He'd looked down at her as she'd curled up, her hands coming up to her breasts, her legs crossing to squeeze every last ounce of fluttering pleasure from her clit. She was the most gorgeous being when she came, her liberated sexuality emanating all around them.

Peg had opened her eyes, a mischievous smile beginning at the corners of her mouth, "I want you...in my mouth *again*."

"Oh?" Gunnar had stepped back, surprised as she came towards him and stood up, grabbing his lats and turning him towards the bed.

"Yes..." Peg had laid him down and gripped his shaft, moving her wet mouth down onto him. Gunnar gasped at how swift and gentle she had handled him.

Peg released him after a moment and reached for her ice water. He'd watched her, his eyes widening as she'd placed ice in her mouth and returned to his cock. In one fell swoop, she slid her mouth down on him again and the ice cube moved along his shaft, causing him to suck his breath between his teeth at the sheer pleasure of her oral play.

"Baby, that feels so fucking good. Oh, my gaw-" He could hardly speak.

Peg smiled and slurped the melting water along his shaft, the warmth of her mouth contrasting with the coolness of the ice.

"Haven't you ever had ice cube sex before?"

Gunnar, unable to speak, shook his head. Peg could tell this was a first for him and she loved pleasuring him. His moans of bliss made her swirl her tongue more, and move her hands along the base of his cock.

"*Peg...*"

She'd smiled again, feeling the last remnants of the ice cube disappear beneath her tongue. She'd increased her rhythm, opening her lips and mouth, feeling him getting close. Gunnar moaned and gently placed his hand on her hair, moving himself deeper in her mouth, losing control.

"Oh, Peg...*don't*...stop...."

Peg felt his climax coming up through his shaft when and suddenly his body shook and hot streams of cum pumped against the roof of her mouth. She'd swallowed slowly, causing him to breathe and moan into her, his body pulsing...then collapsing beneath her mouth. His chest had heaved up and down as she'd sucked him gently until he'd begun to recover. She'd slid her mouth slowly from him to let him rest.

Panting, he'd murmured, "Holy fuck...*babyyyyy*..."

Peg had smiled at him, loving how how good it made her feel to bring him pleasure.

He'd reached down and lifted her under her arms to bring her up to his mouth so he could kiss her and taste his cum in her mouth.

Peg had moved her body up on top of him, pulling his hands over his head and wrapping his fingers around the rungs of the metal bed frame. A smile had appeared across his lips and Peg could tell that he was very pleased with her wanting to ravish him. She'd liked that he looked as if he'd just received the best blow job ever.

"That...*was*..."

Peg had kissed him before he could finish his thought. She'd begun moving her vulva up and down his shaft, teasing. "Do you give consent?"

He'd smiled wider and nodded, liking that she was keeping him aroused with her teasing.

"Are you sureeeee...?" She'd moved slower and soaked him with her slickness.

"Oh my...you are sooo wet, baby..."

"All for you. Are you sure?"

"Like the first time...when you asked me then...*I'm sure*..."

Before he'd finished the sentence, she'd already slid down on him, accepting and surrounding him with her heated womb. Pushing her hands against his chest and sitting upright she began rocking deep and slow on his cock to a rhythm unique to the two of them.

"Oh fuck..." Gunnar's hands had released from the bed frame and gripped her hips to hold on. Peg increased her speed, gliding along the length of him over and over.

Just before he'd lost all control, she'd stopped. He'd opened his eyes looking up at her as if she were the most magnificent creature he'd ever seen. Without a word, she'd climbed off, and turned around, and sunk down on him...in reverse cowgirl.

"O'Clery!"

Gunnar turned, his head snapping towards the startling sound.

"What the fuck, LT, I thought you'd gone deaf." The young agent moved his hand away from Gunnar's shoulder careful not to touch him now that he had his attention.

Gunnar couldn't believe how immersed he'd been in the memory of his time with Peg, and at work, of all places.

"What's up?"

"We're headed out, sir. Oh, and your chief called."

"Oh...oh shit, did he?"

"Yeah."

"Well, that'll have to wait. You all set for this, bud?"

Gunnar stood up, relieved that his erection subsided quickly after his daydreaming had been interrupted. He picked up his gear and headed toward the door, trying to shake off the memory of her and distract himself more with work.

Chapter 15
PROTECTED

Josephine frowned when she noticed a car pull up and park outside her office. She didn't have clients.

A young woman emerged from the tiny Honda. Her hair was pulled back into a bun and the bulge beneath her white blazer suggested she was law enforcement. She reminded Jo of how Aileen had looked when she'd first been hired as an agent.

Josephine relaxed her shoulders a bit and got up from her desk to go to the door. She hoped the woman would just leave the box she was carrying, but no such luck. The knock came softly.

"Yeah?"

Her voice was as soft as her knock, "Uh, yes ma'am. I have a package...err a box for you?"

"How do you know who I am?" Josephine spoke to her through the door letting the cameras record the woman's appearance and responses.

"You are Josephine Adeyo yes?"

"Who's asking?"

"A friend of Aileen Lauden?"

Josephine smiled, realizing Aileen was being cute, sending her some sort of gift. She opened the door and made eye contact with the young woman.

"Yep, that's me."

The agent handed her the box, made eye contact slightly, and turned to go.

"Uh...well, okay. Thank you?" Jo thought her departure abrupt. She looked down at the box, then again at the woman, who was walking back to her Honda. The girl waved, got in, reversed, and left.

Shutting the door, Josephine walked to the reception desk to open the box, hoping desperately it wasn't something embarrassing, as Aileen was known to send crazy gifts. A talking dildo was one of the strangest surprises she'd sent, especially in the middle of a busy shift at the urgent care office. She opened the flaps. Inside was a beautiful gun box with a note folded on top. She opened the cream-colored stationary and read it:

Please give this to Peg. I don't know if she is protected. Can't stand that I left her without one. Thank you for your help putting him away. Please don't mention this is from me.

Jo sat down, looking at the handwritten note that was clearly not from her best friend. He was clever. Feeling sad for Gunnar... and for Peg, she put the note back and closed the box. Her heart ached for these two people who loved each other so much but were unable to be together...for whatever reason.

Richie answered the door with a bright smile that creased the corners of his eyes. He was happy to see Peg had, in fact, made it over in two minutes. Peg handed him a bottle of Jameson.

"Please accept my apology. I usually don't do late. I discovered that I was more exhausted than I thought I was."

Peg furrowed her brows, feeling awful for being over a half hour late.

Richie was impressed with the whiskey. "Oh well, you are certainly forgiven now." He chuckled and stepped out of the way, waving her in.

Peg stepped in and saw a half-decorated house with moving boxes all over. The place was clean and smelled good. Two dogs, one a black lab, the other a brown mixed retriever, came running up. She bent down to greet them the way she did most dogs. They both licked and smelled her.

"Wow, they like you!"

"Dogs and kids often do...it's exes and their families I have no luck with."

He laughed at her dry humor. "I know what you mean."

She hugged and scratched both dogs behind their ears, then followed Richie through the kitchen and out onto the deck where he had set up a table with food and three plates.

She took the seat across from the two plates not sure if he had a girlfriend arriving. Richie grabbed two red solo cups and poured them both a double.

"So, do you have an ex...or just tough in-laws to deal with?"

Richie tapped his cup to hers in a toast, "Tough ex, tough...ex in-laws."

"Oh, I'm sorry."

"I'm not."

He smiled at her and sipped his whiskey.

Peg sat and sipped hers as well. She noticed he was attractive in a tall, dad-bod-guy sort of way. He took care of himself by having a closely-trimmed beard and clean-shaven bald head, and he smelled good. She could tell he shopped at the "big and tall" department at Marshall's and thought that the effort he put into his presentation was admirable.

He sat down across from her and started to pass her food.

"Here, help yourself. I'm sorry it's not still hot."

"Well, that's definitely my fault."

"I'm just glad you made it. I was hoping you weren't one to break promises."

He teased her and passed her more food to put on her plate.

Peg looked up at him before lowering her eyes to the empty plate next to his.

"I don't often break promises. Are you expecting..."

The screen door opened abruptly, and RJ swiftly emerged and slammed it closed behind him. His eyes met hers and he froze as she smiled. Peg suspected he might not have known she was coming.

"Uh, hey."

"Hiya." Peg stood up as he walked toward her with his hand out. She shook it. "You must be RJ."

"Yes ma'am." He tried to look in her eyes but lowered his gaze as a smile crept to one side of his mouth.

Peg didn't think him shy, just surprised. She sat back down watching him throw his book bag to the deck floor. "It's nice to finally meet you."

"Um, you too, ma'am."

"Peg."

RJ looked at his father, who smiled at him and started handing him food. He'd known Richie was inviting Peg over for steaks but had had no idea she was so hot.

"You just coming in from school?"

RJ nodded. "Well, my friend's house. We were studying for this prodigious math test."

Peg looked at him and noticed he'd not only mentioned studying for math but also used a college-level word. She wondered if he was a dedicated student.

"Feeling confident about it?" She bit into a piece of steak that melted in her mouth. It seemed Richie was a good cook.

RJ smiled. He liked her. His own mother didn't give a shit about his grades or interests. "Actually, yes. I'm hoping to ace it. Being new in the class has been...well, challenging. I'm hoping the teacher will see I listen to him."

Richie cut into his food. "He will, son, don't worry. You've always been pretty good at impressing your teachers."

"Let's just hope these are the last ones I need to impress." RJ gave his father a pointed look, and Peg could tell there was a bit of resentment behind it.

Richie looked at her. "My son is not enjoying our third move since Christmas."

She looked between the two. "Will this be the last for awhile or..."

"Yes. I'm actually purchasing this house from the owner once we can get things sorted out."

"Hopefully I'll be able to graduate here and go to college."

"Oh great. Are you interested in our college here?"

RJ nodded. "I am. I think I will be able to start as early as this year. I just have to graduate the early high school first."

Peg concluded that he was super smart. If he was already nearing graduation at fifteen, he was well on his way. "Ah, so you go to Tomahawk?"

"Yes! I only need a few more credits by summer and then I will be able to walk in their graduation."

Richie smiled. "RJ is very excited to move forward at such a young age. He deserves it. He's worked hard despite all our mini setbacks and moves. He's always been a great student. Quick learner."

"Thanks, pops."

Peg smiled. It seemed as if the two took care of each other. She wasn't surprised-that was a dynamic she'd observed before when the maternal parent had let the household down. She knew something like that might have happened since Richie had mentioned an ex. She figured it would come out if they wanted to share. In the meantime, she was enjoying the food and how they interacted with each other. Her shoulders started to relax, and she began to feel relieved that she had decided to come.

"I think you'll do great here then."

"I'm interested in the space program."

Peg nodded. "Excellent choice."

RJ chewed with his mouth shut then spoke, "So Peg, were you really shot?"

She felt a pang of dread but she'd known it was only a matter of time before she would be asked. She looked at Richie, who shrugged. He hadn't told RJ and was hoping she knew that.

"Yup."

"The guys across the street mentioned it. You know that one who is in a wheelchair?"

Richie looked from her to RJ. "When did you talk with them?"

"The other day. I was being neighborly."

Peg knew being neighborly meant gossiping about others. "This town is surprisingly small for such a large population."

"I'm sorry, Peg." Richie nudged his son in the arm. RJ lifted his eyebrows.

"No worries. It was quite a dramatic incident. I'm sure it rocked the neighbors since the neighborhood is normally quiet. I have a crazy ex who decided to shoot me and kidnapped me."

RJ swallowed slow, "Holy shit, are you okay?"

Peg appreciated his concern. "I am. I mean my body is healing, I have a gnarly scar which is the easiest part. The PTSD is much harder to navigate."

"I'm sure." Richie knew more than he led on.

"What happened? Was he is just some like crazy dude?"

Peg exhaled, trying to think of a way to distill the whole situation down to a short version.

"Well RJ, sometimes you marry someone you think is a decent guy, a soldier who fought for his country, a parent to a little girl, someone who wants to be a family and run a martial arts studio together, then years in you find out he didn't even see combat and faked being an army ranger, which is called stolen valor. His daughter can't stand him because he's an awful parent. And that martial arts business? That was a cover for him to inappropriately touch women, young girls, and try to sleep with men. You question your heart and the decisions you make because you realize you believe in others before they show you who they really are. I left him after his best friend told me he was inappropriate with a sixteen-year-old girl in the parking lot of one of our martial art gyms. I just couldn't be married to someone who would hurt someone else's baby. He didn't like that I'd left him and found out his dark secrets. He came to hurt me...but I was rescued, and he was put in a psychiatric hospital in Arizona. So, life is better now... a gift."

"Holy fuck." RJ just stared at her.

Richie did too, then looked at RJ. "Son?"

"Sorry Dad, but seriously that's fucked up.

Richie had had no idea about all that was involved either and suddenly was regretting his decision to help Dereck Law in any capacity...whether he owed the man or not.

osephine knocked on Aileen's door and waited anxiously for her to answer. Aileen scuffled to unlock and open the door, after spying Jo's stressed face. She'd seen all of Jo's expressions at one time or another, and her stressed look was always the most unnerving. She would have preferred to see her angry instead.

"Breathe, my sweet."

"I am breathing, Aileen, just faster than usual." Jo sat down with the package on her lap and waited for Aileen to join her.

"Tell me."

"Well, I'll just show you and you can tell me what you think."

Aileen sat across from her on the chaise and accepted the beautiful wooden box Josephine handed her. Aileen's eyebrows raised as she registered that the artfully-etched, wooden box looked a lot like a gun case. As she opened it and saw the Beretta snug inside the velvet fabric with two full clips, she felt a sense of pride that she hadn't lost her knack.

"Hmmm, okay?"

Jo handed over the accompanying note and waited for her to read it.

Aileen's shoulders dropped. "Oh, wow Jo."

"Right?"

"What are you going to do?"

"*Tell* me what to do."

"I can't." Aileen still didn't want to get involved but was feeling more uncertain about this stance after the time she had spent with Peg recently. She could see how much pain their distance was causing.

"Ai!"

"What's the bigger problem here?"

Jo blinked slow and exhaled, "It's all a big problem. You don't understand how much that woman's heart aches for him."

"He's obviously hurting too."

"Yeah, I'm aware of that. Can't you please help me find him? I know you can find anyone."

Aileen pointed towards Jo's glass of wine, which she'd poured and. Placed on the coffee table. "Yes Jo, I can, but he asked me not to do that. Besides, he's not missing, he wants to not be found, Jo. He's just away on another case and probably trying to get over her."

"Ugh, this man is so frustrating."

"All men are."

"If I bring this to her, she's going to hurt more. If I don't, I am disrespecting that he wants her protected."

"She has guns no?"

Jo nodded. "That asshole ex of hers took her gun out of her truck and shot her with it, remember?"

"Oh, yes. Well, she has others."

"That's not the point Ai, this man sent this to her. It goes deeper than just a weapon for protection. I mean, look at the thing."

Aileen gazed at it again, "It sure is perty...just like Peg."

"Stop that."

Aileen smiled a devilish grin. It was just like her to try to distract Jo from being stressed.

D ereck pushed the last of his urine out, pissed that his dick was acting more like he was ninety than fifty-three. Swatting at a few gnats, he put his cock back in his pants and looked around. He was hidden from the road by the large palm tree trunks and could see the flashers blinking on the mini-van. He needed to return to the vehicle and look pathetic enough to hitch a ride or take someone's car from them, committing yet another crime. He didn't give a fuck at this point, but running out of gas was annoying and not a part of the plan. He had been so excited to have escaped so easily that he hadn't even thought to check the gauge. It wasn't as if he could have stopped to get gas anyway because every station had damn cameras.

He knew his best bet was to carjack some unsuspecting Good Samaritan before they noticed his attire or heard on the radio that he'd escaped from a psychiatric ward. He knew there was most likely a manhunt being coordinated now that a few hours had passed. He needed to find a new way to travel, a way he could stay hidden until he got to her.

Chapter 16

HE'S OUT

Gunnar woke up rock-hard and thinking only of Peg. He still wanted her and it'd been months. He wondered when the excitement, the deep fluttering within his loins, would begin to dissipate. It was slightly unnerving that he continued to think about her so often. The time that had passed hadn't helped him to forget that he loved what she did to him.

He thought about how their connection might border on obsession...one he was trying to deny because she deserved a good life, a calm life with someone who could give her the quality time and significance she deserved.

Gunnar glanced at his phone and saw two more missed calls from the Chief. He dreaded talking to the bastard. He'd put him on this case with the feds to punish him, and now he wanted to talk. He rolled over, not wanting to give his boss the satisfaction of knowing he was miserable. He was growing tired of his life, all the stress, the failure of his marriage, his kids grown and not needing him as much, having to lose Peg. All of it was something he just wanted to push away. He was tired...so very, very tired.

He closed his eyes and there she was again. Her eyes had danced when she smiled, and he'd loved how her blonde hair had shone bright in the dark as she'd hopped out of her truck in shorts and wedge-heeled sandals. He remembered how his cock had hitched in his jeans as he'd looked at her tanned, muscular legs. He hadn't been able to wait to part them and sink into her.

As he'd crossed the street he'd loved the wide smile he'd seen on her face as she looked back at him. Truth-be-told, he had been shocked she had agreed to see him on a Saturday night after dropping her girlfriend at home after the bar. She wasn't much of a drinker, but she was one to give her time wholeheartedly to a friend. He'd walked her to the door with his hand on the small of her back.

"Baby, these shorts. Oh my god, how can I get them on your floor?" He'd let her know that he appreciated how classy yet sexy she dressed. It had turned him on in ways he didn't know how to verbalize.

She'd huffed a laugh while trying to quietly unlock the door so her roommates wouldn't wake. It had only been eleven-thirty, but they'd already been hibernating in their rooms despite it being a weekend.

"I'm glad you like how I'm dressed, that makes me feel good."

"All I want is to make you feel good."

She'd turned, kissing him and smelling the faint aroma of cinnamon mixed with alcohol on his breath, "Ah, I see. Fireball?"

"Yes. I've had a few shots. Forced myself to rest in bed while watching the dogs all day."

"Oh, I see." Peg had lead him into her room in the dark, sensing he had been a different kind of feisty.

He'd locked the door and left the lights off. Then he'd found her in the dark, bringing his mouth down onto hers hard, kissing her in an almost animalistic way. He'd grabbed at her clothing, stripping it off her and throwing it to the floor.

Peg had kicked off her heels just in time, her body falling back onto the bed as he'd pushed her down and positioned himself on top of her. He'd slid his fingers into her slick softness and heard her gasp as he sunk his mouth into the nape of her neck. She had always been so ready for him and he hadn't been able to wait. He'd dreamt of her the whole day and was hard because of it.

Gunnar had stood up, pulling his shirt over his head and pulling his jeans off. Peg had sat up and come towards him, freeing him from his underwear, sliding him slowly into her mouth. His head had fallen back and his hand had wound into her hair to pull her mouth further down his shaft. He hadn't been able to believe how incredible her mouth had felt; it had almost made him explode. The way she'd used her lips, her tongue, and her hands had almost driven him mad. She'd cupped his balls with her other hand and started to increase her rhythm. He'd known he would succumb to her too soon, so he'd reached down and lifted her to standing.

He'd thrown her back on the bed, pressed his face between her legs and kissed her, soaking his mouth with her scent. Peg had cried out, unable to withstand his taunting. He'd been able to feel her getting close.

He'd stood up and pulled her to the edge of the bed, entering her hard and fast. Peg had covered her own mouth-wanting to scream into the darkness but not wanting to wake her roomies.

Gunnar had indulged his animalistic side and had pulled at her hips while pounding into her sweet, slickness. He'd begun fucking her in a way he hadn't before and had slammed into her over and over, creating a slapping noise both had not been accustomed to hearing.

"Oh my...god...." Peg had whispered, looking up at him, her eyebrows furrowing, her body succumbing to his every thrust.

"Alcohol makes me want to just keep going, baby. You feel so fucking good."

Peg had tried to grab at the sheets, unable to process so much pleasure rushing through her body. She'd felt she had no control and yet had wanted none because it'd felt so fierce and gratifying.

"I..."

Gunnar had smiled, looking down at her and loving that he was giving her so much satisfaction. He'd thought she was the most beautiful, sexual creature he'd ever met.

"Yes?"

"I...think. I...think I might die."

Gunnar had leaned forward and paused, whispering into her ear, "That's okay baby, I know how to revive you. I'm certified in CPR."

Peg had giggled at the joke, knowing that he had the same first responder training as she did. She'd loved his sense of humor.

Gunnar had straightened up and continued his deep, fierce thrusts. She'd reached up to touch his chest, watching him rail her in ways that made her body surrender.

"I'd fuck you back to life baby...because I need your soul."

Gunnar's cell buzzed annoyingly on the nightstand. He was disappointed to see his boss was calling for a fourth time and forcing him to return to the present.

"O'Clery." Gunnar's voice was gruff.

"He's out."

"What?"

Gunnar's boss grumbled, annoyed he had to repeat himself after calling so many times. "Your gal's ex. He escaped. Murdered an orderly and took his vehicle."

"You've got to be fuckin' kidding me!"

"I'm sending your replacement. Get your ass back to Las Ramas, we've got a manhunt on our hands and you know he's coming for her...*and you.*"

Gunnar hung up the phone and jumped out of bed, thinking only of Peg and her safety.

Dereck drove up the dirt road and turned onto the paved street. He looked back in the rearview mirror, smirking as he left the minivan behind, the flashers still on. Luring Minnie and Walter Sikes to help him with his fake flat tire scheme had been too easy. Killing them both with the crowbar in the desert had been even easier.

He remembered a time when he'd liked elderly people. Now, he just wanted everyone to get out of the fucking way so he could get to Peg.

It had been a long time since he'd felt this dark...killing-urge thing. He hadn't been good at it in combat, could never quite pull the trigger except for that one day in Kosovo when that woman and her kid ran out that door to escape and he'd put a bullet in both. He'd wanted to be a hero and had instead wound up killing two innocent people. He had waited all that time and when he'd finally got the nerve, he'd ended up making a mess. Another dark secret to shove down. He remembered how lucky he was none of the other soldiers had known it had been him.

Turning it into fuel, he knew he hadn't been able to kill Peg before but now, *now* it was a must. He absolutely could not wait to see her dead eyes. He yearned for it with his whole body.

Pressing on the pedal he accelerated toward home...her home next door to Richie.

P eg heard her phone vibrate. She thought about ignoring it but worried it might be her daughter or son. She hadn't talked to either in a week and needed to catch up. However, it was Josephine.

Josephine's Cell:
Got a sec?

Peg's Cell:
Of course. You ok?

Yes. I'm here.

Oh?

Aileen told me your address. I'm sorry to impose but, I have to talk to you.

I'll be right there.

***

Peg opened the screen door and met Josephine's gaze. Josephine pursed her lips and tried to smile at Peg as she stepped in past her. Peg then motioned for her to enter her bedroom and closed the door behind them.

Peg noticed that Josephine was holding a box as she sat down on her futon couch, looking up at her. She thought Peg looked beautiful, her hair a bit tossed and her eyes sleepy. She felt nervous but forced herself to start to explain.

"I want you to have this. I don't remember if you said you were carrying, and I've been feeling uneasy lately. Please sit."

Peg frowned, feeling a bit confused but she sat on the chaise lounge and took the box Jo handed her. She could tell it was a a gun box, a beautiful one at that. Considering that Jo was pro-carry, she wasn't too shocked at the gift. She opened it and a pang of pain surged through her heart as it was a Beretta-it made her think of Gunnar.

"Oh, wow Jo, this is-"

"I couldn't remember if you still had the gun from your truck."

"No. Wouldn't want it anyway...I didn't even save the bullet he put through me. I let the cops keep it all."

Jo sat back against the couch feeling she was in the clear, "So, you'll use this?"

"Well sure, and thank you. Where did you find such a beauty... it looks lik-" Peg shut down before finishing her thought. Her heart felt heavy again.

"Oh, I have another. I just want to know you have one on you."

"I appreciate that so much, Jo. This is so thoughtful."

"I hope you never have to even unholster it, girl."

Peg huffed. "Yeah. I'd actually love to get through this whole journey of mine without ever having to point it at another person."

"What was it like when you were in law enforcement?" Jo wanted to move on from the thought of Gunnar and more to Peg's thoughts.

"Thankfully, I only had to threaten. I wasn't in long before my ex ruined things. Actually, this damn CPTSD got me and it's still getting me."

Jo shook her head. "I don't know Peg, with all you've been through I still think you're one of the more well adjusted women I've ever known." Jo meant it. Peg was top notch in her book. She felt a moment of guilt for not disclosing the truth about where she'd gotten the gun.

"You're very kind. Perhaps I project calm on the outside."

"Well, I still think you process well. It's all in how we move through it."

Peg smiled. "I'd like to not have to 'move through' anything for a long, long while."

(Hours Later)

***

Peg's Journal Entry:

Today was interesting. I got a text and then a visit from Jo. She stopped by and gifted me a beautiful Baretta in an artfully etched box with black velvet fabric inside. The gun was loaded and came with two full clips. She was concerned for my safety, which was nice to hear, and couldn't remember if I had a firearm. I let the cops keep everything. I don't want the memories. I love this gun as it looks like something Gunnar would have given me. I accepted it and talked with her awhile then placed it under my chaise lounge.

I had dinner over at Richie's with him and his son, RJ. It was pleasant. His kid did ask me about being shot but I wasn't shocked. Everyone in this neighborhood is curious about the woman shot in the doorway then kidnapped by her crazy ex. I'm sure most can't believe I'm still living here. I really should head back to my house but something inside me doesn't want to go there yet. I honestly don't want to see what a shithole he made out of our family home. Ugh, I'm just so over Dereck Law even having existence. Horrible human. Can't believe I once picked him and thought he was a stunt guy. Gunnar makes him look like a clown.

On a lighter note, I've been dreaming of Gunnar every night. I miss him so much and notice I find comfort in thinking of our memories together. It feels like a present death. He's still out there but I'm here mourning him and wanting to spend every moment together with him...well, because life is fucking short.

The last dream was about our first time sixty-nineing. It was that time, early on in our "situationship", when he walked into my room a little after nine in the morning. He touched my body, running his hands along my tush and arch of my back. He looked so hot, his chest broad, waist trim...a newly-grown goatee that felt good trailing along my skin as he kissed my shoulders and back!

He removed his clothing in between caressing my tummy, my breasts, and my neck. I liked his touch. He was always very gentle but intense. He was already hard for me, which was an incredible turn-on. He whispered how much he wanted me, how beautiful he thought I was. I was soaked before he even made it across the room to touch me, but his words ignited me.

He kissed me deep and my hand wrapped around his hard, warm cock. His body felt so good on mine, especially since the overhead fan had chilled me while I was lying naked, and his warmth radiated through me. His connection overtook me, and I slipped my tongue in his mouth tasting his sweetness. I slid my hand into his underwear to feel him more, and he stood up to take them off. I turned myself so my head hung slightly off the edge of the bed upside down and pulled him into my mouth. The sounds that escaped his mouth confirmed I was pleasuring him in a way he'd never experienced.

He murmured my name and laid on me so his mouth was between my legs, sending surges of pleasure throughout my body. I took more of him into my mouth and sucked slow and lovingly along his shaft. We were in a glorious sixty-nine position, and it was so gentle and comfortable, we were devouring each other staying in our slow rhythm and feeling the exquisite delectation.........

We moved to missionary so he could face me. Initial entry was such a fucking turn-on. We eased into it. As much as my body responded to him and was always ready, I was always too small for his size at first, and this made it all the more blissful! He'd go quiet while burying himself inside me... and I'd gasp no matter how much I tried to stifle it.

My body wanted him and gripped and squeezed him as if it had been missing him. I pushed towards him and could feel him all the way to my cervix! Aching pleasure shot up through my womb and chakras. I couldn't explain it, but I'd never enjoyed a man's body, or energy, as much as Gunnar's. There was just something about him, about how he moved in the world...moved within my body.

I remember he guided us into an amazing rhythm and then started whispering, "Do you like being made love too?"

I could hardly speak, but I nodded. He commented, "I wonder how this would feel for an entire weekend, at the hot springs."

I smiled, still unable to think straight because of how damn good he felt thrusting into me. Every now and again, he'd arch and press harder on the end making me gasp loudly. I laughed because he'd tease, playing with my body, making me want more.

He suddenly admitted, "I can't believe how tight your pussy is; I can't get enough of you." I felt flattered and, as I'd moved on top of him, he said, "I have never had anyone ride me like you...like this."

I looked down smiling and put a little more rocking and slow squeezing into my movements.

I remember how he once told me he was "a simple guy" and "very vanilla", which surprised me because I've experienced him EXTREMELY ADVENTUROUS. He smiled then and gripped my hips more encouraging me to grind deeper and slower. I'm honored to have shared such pleasure with him. We had the kind of sex I'd dreamt about for years. I didn't know how to even explain that to him, so I just showed him. Every chance I could.

I moved into reverse cowgirl upon his request, and after a while, he took me from behind and also on our sides when it was time to rest. I enjoy that nothing was rushed and each position felt as if it flowed into the next. He had amazing control to hold out, and I could tell he really enjoyed spending time in each position, getting as much pleasure as we could out of it.

I remember feeling him get close when I was in reverse cowgirl, and I circled my hips for him to add a little "extra". He spread my tush open and mentioned our slickness and how beautiful what we do looked. It made me want to please him more and more.

He did eventually let go, cumming and cumming...and cumming as I moved on him. I timed it with how his hands grasped at me and then slightly started to relax. He was quiet, and as he crashed over and then relaxed, I eased my thrusts.

I slid off and turned around to lay down and let him recover, but he motioned for me to ride him more, wanting to see me. I eased down on him and rocked keeping him hard while watching his sleepy bedroom eyes. He looked up at me watching me slowly coax his dick into staying hard.

He asked, "Was it odd to have me cum in your mouth last time after so many years of never swallowing him?" He was referring to Dereck and how I would spit his cum in a tissue or go to the bathroom and spit it out in the sink. I was surprised he'd remembered I'd told him that, but I told him the truth and mentioned how something in me knew Dereck didn't deserve it... not like him.

"I wanted to with you" I said softly. Which was the truth. I really enjoy pleasing him; I want him to know I felt he was worthy...good enough, even if he had a hard time believing in himself.

I woke up feeling yearning for him inside me. God I miss this man so much. I'll never understand why he left.

Chapter 17

CHUBBY

Richie rinsed a dish in the sink, feeling the suds on his skin and wondering how Peg would feel on his skin. He'd been dreaming of her lately and had tried to stop but after her visit, something had begun gnawing at him. He did not believe Dereck's tale of woe anymore, especially after hearing Peg's side of the story and some of the things he'd done to her. He knew in his gut Dereck was a horrible person. He had, after all, fucked Richie's wife and told him it was for his own good. He also told him not to fall for Peg. That was not working so well.

He imagined her at the sink in front of him, bent slightly forward, her hands in the hot water, her gorgeous ass lifted in the wedge heels she wore. He could feel himself getting hard and pressing into her. He wanted to feel her push back, moan in that beautiful, melodious voice she had, asking him if they could "take this to your room"-to which he would reply with an enthusiastic affirmative.

He imagined feeling her in his arms, her legs draped over his arm as he carried her up the stairs, her mouth still on his, her arms around his neck, giving herself to him so easily. It had been years since he'd felt a woman wanting him. He was eager to slowly undress her, touch her skin, her pussy, bury his face between her thighs and hear her cry out for him. He wanted to feel her pull him into her and experience her slick, wet womb engulf him with desire.

"Dad!"

Richie's shoulders shrugged as he jumped, "What!?"

RJ smiled, watching his father try to grab at the utensils he'd dropped in the water. "Jeezus, I've been talking to you for a whole minute straight. What's wrong with you?"

"Nothing. I heard you."

"Oh really? How was she?"

"Who?"

"Whoever gave you that chubby." RJ backed up pointing at his father's crotch.

"RJ, go the fuck to bed would ya!"

"Seems like I should be sending you to bed, Dad. You might hurt yourself with that."

Richie turned back toward the sink to finish the dishes. "Get lost kid. I don't need your harassment."

"What's wrong Pops, tables turned? Don't you remember you and Mom teasing the shit out of me when I was eight?"

"That was all your mom, kid."

RJ leaned against the wall, out of Richie's reach in case he needed to run. He enjoyed teasing this father like this.

"Maybe...but you could have stopped her. She bullied me right in front of you."

"I let her have it when we were alone. She was well aware that bodies were not to be made fun of."

"Mom's a dick."

"I have no comment, but we don't have to worry about that now. She's in another state."

"True. So speaking of, is yours standing at attention because our hot neighbor came over and you can imagine things better now....her lips, that ass..."

"RJ!"

Richie turned quick but RJ was younger and faster. He ran up the stairs laughing hysterically.

"I knew it!!! You've got a crush on Peg Law...you horny old man you!"

Richie sighed, a small smile appearing at the corners of his mouth.

Dereck parked the Sikes' old beat up jalopy a few streets over and in the dessert behind some dark shrubbery. He waited there, deciding that he would gain entry to Richie's house in the morning after he drove his brat kid to school. He knew he could sleep in Richie's back yard because the man never let his dogs stay out at night for fear they would bark. He hoped he wouldn't have to kill his mutts but was ready if he had to. They'd liked him last time he was with them. Most dogs like him for some reason. He hoped the was still true.

Unfortunately the manhunt had ensued and it was only a matter of time before the authorities came to talk to Peg, if they hadn't already. He planned to stay in Richie's spare room for as many days as he could without being detected. He wanted to watch her, watch Gunnar. He'd kill Richie and his kid if he had to, but he was exhausted. He would prefer to save his energy for Peg and Gunnar. He might even get to lay them out and get away with it. If not, he wanted to make sure they all died together. His mood shifted, excitement in the pit of his belly. He was getting closer to achieving his goal.

Gunnar pulled into his driveway, his heart pounding. He didn't want another confrontation with his ex, although he missed his daughter. Sitting there, he stared at the home he'd never much liked. The memories of raising his kids there had made it worth the money. He struggled with wanting to go inside and wrap his arms around his last born. He wanted to feel her squeeze his neck and whisper how much she missed and loved him-it would calm him.

He thought of Peg. He had to get to her. He'd put her last in so many ways; he didn't feel right about doing it for another moment.

Gunnar's Cell:
Hey baby girl. You up?

Libby's Cell:
Hi Dad. I'm in bed. I studied for my test though, like you said.

Great job sweetie. I love you.

Love you more Dad. I'll text you tomorrow after math. I think I'll do well.

I know you will. Nite-

Goodnight.

Gunnar felt better knowing his daughter was safe. He decided not to go in and have to listen to his ex scream at him. She'd gotten so very angry in the last few weeks since receiving the divorce papers. He was giving her everything, but that was not what she wanted. It would take more time to ease twenty-six years of marriage. He had tried to continue on after finding out he was not the biological father of his older two children...but it was the kiss of death for the marriage. He could never see her the same again. She broke him. Peg healed. He knew his future was Peg.

He backed out with his headlights still off and pulled away. He was going to have to watch Peg's house for the night and try not to dream of all she'd do to him if he were in her room with her. God how he loved the woman.

***

Chapter 18

AWAY

Dereck stared down the street at Peg. It was getting dark, but he'd decided to wait until there was no light before breaking into Richie's house. He thought he might catch a glimpse of her but had had no idea she would look so damn good. He'd shot her and apparently, it had only made her stronger. *Fuck!*

She hopped down out of her truck, her tight ass bouncing slightly making his dick hitch. He was annoyed she still had that effect on him! He leaned back squinting, a groan escaping his throat, more from disdain than want. He knew that if he continued to watch her he'd get hard, but he couldn't look away.

Shifting in his seat he leaned forward to see more details. Her hair was blonder, longer too. Her muscles were more defined. That pissed him off because it probably meant Gunnar had been working out with her. He probably wanted her strong because of how easily it had been to overpower her previously.

Dereck had thought about going after Gunnar's wife and kids but he'd reckoned he was probably divorced and focusing on killing him. He sat back again as she disappeared into the house. He hoped Gunnar would show soon. He'd like to see him and know they were right next door as he hid in Richie's house.

Smiling, he realized how exciting it felt to be out of the psych prison they'd put him in-he was back in control. His targets were completely unaware of how close to death they were. How was he going to take everything from them when he felt like it and they'd be entirely at his mercy.

Dereck chuckled deep within his chest, an evil, breathy sound, his eyes glazed over. He didn't even care that he'd lose his life too. As long as he took them both out with him he'd be happy...

Gunnar picked up the call on the second ring. He'd known he'd hear from her.

"Agent Lauden?"

Aileen loved his voice and that he was always respectful, "You knew I couldn't stay away huh?"

"Tense times."

"So, you know he's out?"

"I'm back because he is."

Aileen's eyebrows raised, "You're with her?"

"No."

"O'Clery...go to her."

Gunnar ran his hand over his bald head and leaned back in his chair, "I can't see her Aileen. She deserves peace and..."

"You love her."

He paused, "I-"

"Fucking-A Gunnar! What the hell is wrong with you? People like us don't always get this chance, you goddamn know that."

Aileen's voice was relatively calm but she wanted to remind him that he was lucky. There wasn't a lot of love in law enforcement. She wanted to remind him that he shouldn't dismiss his opportunity to grasp it.

Gunnar couldn't speak. He didn't know how to argue about this.

"That woman loves you. She loves you in a way that makes us all want it. She's so broken without you. Jo and I have seen her just existing. Don't you know this? You just walked out of her life."

He raised his voice a bit. "It was for her own good. I have nothing to offer her!"

"SHE'S NOT THAT KIND OF WOMAN! Gunnar, he was always going to come after her. Look at her, she's a light in this world.

He's a dark evil that wants to put that out. She just wanted what every woman wants. Love. She wants *your* love Gunnar. The real shit. That deep-down unending love. The kind that spans lifetimes, my guy. It's not often that happens. You know this. The shit we've seen proves real love is elusive. Why won't you go to her?"

He remained quiet. He didn't know how to respond.

"Have you at least contacted her to let her know he escaped?"

"No. I have men on it. I...*can't*...see her."

"Why?"

"I just-"

"Gunnar, what the fuck is wrong with you?"

"I don't know Aileen. I'm afraid."

She huffed a small laugh. "More comfortable in an adrenaline-filled fire fight than seeing the woman that captured your heart, huh?"

Gunnar knew it was fucked up. "Something like that."

"What if he gets her? What if you never see her again."

"Stop. I'm not going to let that happen."

Aileen was not going to let up. "No really. What if-"

"I won't let that *happen*."

"Well, what he gets her again? You know he's worse, right? What if he-"

Gunnar exhaled, "I...*won't let that happen*."

"The manhunt the last few days has brought nothing. You know he's probably already here."

"He's a damn fool if he is."

"He's a psycho Gunnar."

"True. Did you and Jo give her the gun?"

"She has it."

"Good."

Aileen had to know. "Why didn't you want her to know it was from you?" She would have at least felt you cared."

"Let me give you a call back. The chief is trying to get a hold of me."

Aileen softened her voice. "Take care and be safe bud."

P eg stepped into her room and saw the gun box on the chaise lounge. She couldn't shake the heavy feeling that something was wrong. She picked it up but instead of putting it under the chair to hide it again she placed it back down and put a pillow over it. Something told her to keep it close. She turned to get her overnight bag and was happy to be heading to her daughter's to watch her grandson while his parents took a night away for themselves. The world seemed gentler when she was with her grandson, and she looked forward to their time together.

Her phone beeped with an incoming text:

Aileen's Cell:
Hey there. You have any time to talk?

Peg's Cell:
Sure, just packing to go see my grandson

Oh. Can you stop by?

I was going to head out of town in an hour. Everything ok?

Um, have you talked to Jo?

You're scaring me Aileen, Jo stopped by the other day. What's going on? Have you heard from him. Oh, please...please tell me he's ok.

It's about your ex

Oh fuck. What now?

He's worse. Can you swing by. Getting out of town may be a good idea.

Ok shit. Give me a few.

J osephine heard her cell ding and knew it was a text from Aileen. Things were getting tense. With Gunnar out of the picture, Dereck assumed back, and all of LRPD on the lookout for him, she feared Peg only had her and Aileen to help her.

<u>Aileen's Cell:</u>
Hey

<u>*Jo's Cell:*</u>
You talk to him

Yep. He's back alright but laying low.

So he knows? Hasn't gone to her?

Yes, he came back to hunt Dereck. I don't know how he managed that. His boss punished him for this last time. He has not gone to her. I'm going to have her come here.

That's probably a really good idea Ai, and you can watch her house in case he hides out there up the street from you. What is wrong with O'Clery?!!!

That man feels as if her life is better without him. He says he has nothing to offer her.

Never thought of Peg as someone to demand or want anything...but him.

I think that's the issue Jo, She's not what he's used to. He lives a life where people lie to him every day, where his wife had cheated on him with a coworker, where he only feels worth anything if he is creating

136

solutions. Peg doesn't ask for solutions. She just wants to be able to love him and trust a man.

Maybe he knows he can't give her that. Cop life isn't about honesty and providing time and attention. He may feel like shit every time he thinks of her because he can't figure out how to just give her a simple life. She does deserve peace.

True. But I think it's more than that. There's something keeping him away.

Well Ai, sometimes we have to love someone enough to set them free from our dysfunction.

True. You coming by?

Yep.

Chapter 19

SPEECHLESS

Peg fastened her seatbelt and put the truck in drive to head towards Aileen's house. She was nervous because, although Aileen was great, conversations with her tended to be intense. She also didn't relish driving through her old neighborhood on the way to Aileen's house. Seeing it made her heart hurt.

She knew she needed to decide about moving back to the house soon or just selling it. Thinking of the beauty there, how she'd decorated it and made it a warm, welcoming home brought a smile to her face. She thought of her hammock in the courtyard and how she used to sway in it, looking up at the clouds and wishing for a man who could truly love her.

Her mind shifted to Gunnar. She imagined him walking towards her as she lay on her king-size bed. She'd loved the sultry look in he'd had in his eyes sometimes. It was part of an expression reserved only for her. It would appear on his face as his deep hunger would erupt and his cock hardened. He'd see her black panties and matching bra but, he'd only begin to moan when he noticed the black heels that completed his favorite look of her outfits. She smiled, remembering how he'd placed his hands on her tush and softly murmured. "Ohhhhh my gosh, you look so....."

"Hiiiii. You like? Please touch meeeee...." She remembered begging because of how she'd yearned for the caresses from his strong, warm hands.

He'd nod. "Mmmmm...oh I likes, very...very much..."

Peg steered her truck around a corner as she thought about how Gunnar would roll her over and press down onto her body, kissing her mouth, exploring it with his warm, eager tongue. He'd hug her and meld their bodies together, pressing his engorged dick in between her legs, sure to put just enough pressure onto her clit to make her gasp. He'd hear her voice, enjoy her submission, and would reward her by sliding down her body to pull her panties off and pleasure her vulva with his soft mouth.

Peg's insides quivered as she recalled how she would squirm on the bed as he'd send sheer bliss through her. She would get. So wet that he wouldn't be able to wait to enter her.

She thought of an occasion when he had stood up, disrobing and gazing down at her. He'd crouched down and opened her legs with his thighs. He'd buried himself deep within her, causing her to cry out in ecstasy.

"Oh, Peg...baby...you are so..." Gunnar had groaned as he'd begun the deep, slow thrusts she loved so much.

"I am...all for *you*......." she'd whispered breathlessly.

Gunner had thrust deeper into her, and again. She'd moved her hands down to his rear and pulled him in closer. He'd loved how she wanted him.

The truck rolled to a slow stop at a traffic light and more flashed through her mind. She could almost feel the warm coarseness of his palm as he'd run it from behind her ear, down her neck to her breast, taking it gently into his hand as he'd looked deep into her eyes.

He would bend her slowly onto the bed, enter her from behind and run his hand down her spine sending tingles of exhilaration up through her body, then run his hand through her hair, still thrusting, taking them into a rhythm both their bodies longed for.

Peg heard a horn blare. She accelerated, realizing she was getting lost in the memories of them. It was as if her mind could only calm if she was thinking of him, yet the ache within her heart was brutal after she did.

Sighing she used her blinker and moved up and in front of another car. Aileen lived on the other side of town, so she had to take the highway instead of the backroads as she'd prefer. She always liked the backroads because it was easier to clear her mind and watch to see if Dereck was following behind her. Admittedly, she still kept an eye out for him. Her stomach turned as she thought of how horrible of a person he'd turned out to be. He'd gotten worse as the years progressed.

A pang of fear rushed through her when. She pictured him shooting at her, which was stacked on all the years of bullshit she'd experienced in. Her marriage. She shook her head and huffed, thinking "You only brought pain to this world...to my world. Useless fuck...useless flesh."

Peg could feel anger begin and she didn't want to go there. Anger wasn't her go-to emotion. She quickly pushed Gunnar back into her mind as she put her blinker on and exited the highway to where Aileen and *SHE* lived.

She didn't want to think about the pressures of the house. She shifted again to Gunnar, his body, watching him undress, flinging his clothes away from his gorgeous muscles. Coming towards her waiting on the bed, sliding his arms under her as he slid between her legs, taking all of her. She'd loved surrendering to him.

Her mind grasped at the memory of the time he'd pushed her down on the futon couch and removed her pajama shorts so he could part her legs and lean in to taste and suck.

Peg had whimpered at the sheer pleasure he brought to her, and just before she'd started to build to her first orgasm, he'd retreated taking off his clothes. He'd moved forward, opening her with this engorged cock and had slid right in until he could go no further. He was sure to grind at the end of each stroke, tantalizing her clit with his pelvic bone.

Peg had cried out breathlessly and he'd loved the sound of her voice in his ear. He'd pressed in hard again, and again, listening to her sounds and melding to her body while his rocked to her rhythm.

As she'd gotten close again, he'd released and stood up, pulling her hand to him. He'd wanted to tease her more, but she'd seized the opportunity to kneel down and take him into her mouth, making sure to be gentle. She'd swirled her tongue around his shaft and then up to his tip.

Then it had been his turn to lose his breath and she'd absolutely loved the gentle way he'd cupped her head in his palm and moved her hair so he had a better view.

Before he'd started to lose control, Peg had stood up, wanting to push him down and take him further into her mouth, but he had been too swift. He'd changed positions. So. That he was sitting on the couch with her hips in his palms. He'd pulled her down onto his lap and filled her slickness with his fevered, hard dick. Peg had gasped at the pleasure of mounting him this way. She'd grabbed his thighs to hold on as she'd begun to rock her hips and glide along his lap, shocking them both with how good it had felt to be in the position right in the middle of the room.

"Oh my god, you are beautiful, your back muscles are moving under your tanned skin."

She'd smiled. "You make me feel so good about my body, baby."

"You make me feel good when you share this body with me."

"I love sharing."

He'd smiled then, "Whose pussy is this, baby?"

"All yours. I only give it to you."

Gunnar had loved it when she'd said that and he'd pulled her back to lie on his chest, running his hands up her tummy and cupping her breasts while sucking at the back of her neck. Peg's breath had hitched as delicious chills ran up her spine while his still-hard cock rested inside her.

A few moments later she'd sat up and begun rocking more purposefully, really moving on him.

"I've never been fucked the way you fuck me, baby."

Peg had got him to the edge, stopped, and stood up, turning to see his eyes half-open, a confused expression on. His face. She'd reached out to help him up. He'd stood but, instead of going to the bed, he'd stepped toward her vodka.

"I'm going to take a swig of your vodka."

"Okay, I hope you like cherries-it's flavored."

He'd smirked while swallowing. Then he'd looked at her sideways. "I like yours."

Peg had giggled at his quick wit and reached for the bottle, taking a sip as well.

Gunnar had stretched out along the bed looking at her. "Lie in my arms?"

"Oh my, someone is snuggly today."

"I am very snuggly today."

"I love that."

He'd pulled her her back up against his chest and let his fingers begin to wander down the front her body and down to her vulva, wandering further as she'd opened her legs, letting him do as he

142

desired. She'd loved the gentle way he'd touched her, never hurting her.

"I love how soaked you get."

Before she had been able to respond, he'd lifted up, laying her on her back and parting her legs so he could enter her.

"May I grow hard inside you?"

"I do like when you do so...but I believe you are already hard.

She'd lost her breath at his deep thrust inside her.

"Uh, yup. I just love the feeling of getting harder for you inside."

"I love it too."

"Yeah?"

"Yes."

"What else do you love?" He'd looked down into her eyes, not wanting her to look away.

Peg had looked up at him, wondering if he was teasing. She'd noticed a pattern of him wanting to hear her profess her love in words despite him not reciprocating. She'd half-smiled, trying to read him.

He'd looked deep into her eyes, knowing her heart. He'd loved her soul and how she'd worn her heart out on her sleeve. He'd leaned in before she could say anything and kissed her...then again...and again. Gunnar had felt safe to be intense and vulnerable and had continued to kiss her. He'd wanted to tell her he loved her but had tried to show her with his body when words failed him.

He'd looked again at her. "Whose pussy is this?"

"All yours-"

"Why, baby?"

Peg had searched his gaze.

He'd smiled. "Why baby?"

She'd relented, *"Because I love you."*

He'd smiled more and thrust harder. "Why?"

"I love you, Gunnar."

He wrapped his arms tighter around her, exploding inside her.

Peg pulled into Aileen's driveway. Before she could turn off the truck, the garage door opened, and she saw Aileen wave her in to park beside her little BMW. Peg did as directed, confused but happy to be able to hide her truck from her old neighbors, who might recognize her vehicle.

Aileen handed her a tall glass of ice tea. "So sweets, there's a multi-state manhunt because your asshole ex killed an orderly, stole his vehicle, and escaped the psych hospital in Arizona."

"What the fuck!?"

Peg put down her glass so she wouldn't drop it. Her body shook and a cold sweat washed over her as she tried to accept the horror. The man she'd been rescued from was now a murderer and most likely planning on heading her way.

"I'm sorry. Does he know where your grandson and daughter live? I'm thinking it's good you get out of town."

"Uh...I don't think he does, no. Oh my god, did he really hurt someone else?"

"Not hurt, *killed* Peg. He's always had it in him; it just surfaced in a more restrictive environment. Have you noticed anything unusual? Have you seen any strangers in your neighborhood or seen anyone following you?"

Peg shook her head. "No. I can't go through this shit again Aileen. I'm just getting back on my feet after him shooting me... and *kidnapping* me."

This time Gunnar wasn't around. He'd left. The abandonment felt like something heavy on her chest.

"I know, Peg. Would you mind if I put a friend of mine on you? They could tail you and watch over you and your family? Or, better yet, can you just hang out here for a while? That's why I wanted you to park in my garage. Jo and I would feel better if you stayed here for a bit. I already have a camera on your house. We could watch to see if he sneaks in and hides there."

Peg's eyes moved from Aileen to the glass of ice tea. She hated this and didn't want to bring any of it to her grandson and daughter. She knew hiding out with Aileen was probably better since she was a genius with hacking into the street cameras and watching everyone around. With Gunnar gone and Dereck knowing exactly where to find her, she considered Aileen's idea.

"I-"

"I'm pretty sure it's your best option until we know more. I have a call into some friends at LRPD. They don't have Dereck's whereabouts yet, but timing suggests he's also killed an elderly couple and taken their car, which could put him here in town, as of last night."

"Oh my god."

"I'm sure officers are looking to speak with you. My guess is Gunnar may have them offering you witness protection soon. This is serious."

"You've heard from him?! Gunnar? You've talked with him??"

"He came back when he was notified of Dereck's escape."

Peg slumped back against the sofa, speechless. Her heart aching.

unnar hung up. He was even more nervous. His officers had not found Peg, and she was not on her way to a safe house as he'd hoped. Her roommates hadn't opened the door but had told an officer through the ring camera that she'd left for the weekend. Her grandson was in Alma, so she may have gone there. He didn't know if Dereck would know about that.

Her truck was gone, but Gunnar was terrified she'd told her roomies she was away because Dereck may have forced her to do so under duress. His mind was all over the place and he had to know more.

He picked up his keys and headed to his truck. He was going to get more intel from the roommates in his own way. He knew they knew who he was. He hoped they'd remember that he'd rescued Peg.

Clicking his seatbelt and running his hand over his bald head, he prayed he wouldn't have to rescue her again. Dereck Law was now a serial killer. He wished he'd taken him out for good.

On his way to her house, he accelerated and flicked on lights and sirens. He looked down at his cell and texted Aileen, just in case, hoping she'd look at her phone and respond or at least be able to help with the cameras.

Chapter 20

BEG

Dereck cursed under his breath staring out the window at Gunnar. He'd managed to make it past one of Richie's dogs, who liked him, but when the second one growled a little too fiercely, he took him out and dumped him over into the other neighbor's yard.

He'd hoped that once Richie discovered the dead dog, he'd be distracted and not focused enough to find him hiding out in the spare room's closet. If he did find him, Dereck was ready to take him out too. He'd start with his bum left knee. As with most tall guys, Richie had a knee injury, and Dereck knew just what to do to him to get his head to lower. He thought about RJ too. He liked the kid, but he was too loyal to his father. Dereck decided he'd take him out quickly as well...but only if he had to.

It annoyed him profusely that Gunnar was even more ripped than he had remembered. The guy was a specimen of muscle-the kind you start developing in high school football and wrestling and just continue building until your body knows no other way of being. Dereck could imagine how much Peg enjoyed Gunnar. They'd probably fuck for hours and do all the things he knew she loved.

He watched Gunnar walk to the door, and he seethed with hatred. Killing Gunnar in front of Peg was going to be the highlight of his life. Hearing her scream would be music to his ears and he vowed to allow it until she was filled with enough desperation and grief, she'd beg him to kill her!

Gunnar pressed the button again and again. He knew Peg's roommates were not going to answer. They were the types to fear cops unless they needed them. He took a chance and spoke as calmly as he could.

"Please uh-Rena? Please help me keep Peg safe. Her ex is after her again and I need to get her to a safe place."

He could hear clicking and shuffling. He waited another full minute. Finally, she responded.

"She's not here O'Clery. What do you mean he's after her again?"

He leaned in so the other neighbors wouldn't hear him. "You haven't seen the news? I need to talk with Peg and get her to a safe place until we apprehend him. Please tell me where she is."

"Great! He fucking knows where we live. Great job LRPD. Again! Call her kid. She'll know where Peg went."

Gunnar lowered his eyes. He felt bad because he could hear the disgust in Rena's quivering voice.

"I'll make sure you're safe, ma'am. We have people on it."

"Yeah, okay, good day, sir."

"Thank you."

Gunnar walked away surveying the neighborhood. He wasn't going to get much more out of Peg's angry roommate. He hoped she didn't throw Peg out after this. One shooting in her home was surely more than enough. He could understand the rage.

Richie didn't understand why Peg wasn't texting him back. He was getting nervous that he had offended her somehow.

Richie's Cell:
I enjoyed our time the other night.

148

(next day)

How are you holding up?

(hours later)

Peg?

(hour later)

Did I say something wrong?

Richie threw his cell down on the counter as he heard the screams of the little girl that lived next door. It wasn't a normal playing-in-the-yard type of scream. It was blood-curdling. He ran out the back door.

P eg looked at Richie's texts and decided no response was the best she could do under the stress she was feeling. She lay back on Aileen's couch. Her mind was racing as she looked up at the ceiling. She couldn't believe she was actually divorcing a serial-killer-R.Kelly-wannabe. As if him wanting underage girls and boys wasn't bad enough, he was now murdering people until he hunted her down.

Could she have really been so stupid as to believe he was a decent person? She pressed her hands to her face and fought the urge to scream into them. Aileen had gone to her office to check the monitors and cameras she had all over the neighborhood; hearing Peg scream would certainly disrupt her progress.

Peg turned over onto her stomach to try to calm her central nervous system. She felt the seem of her jeans caress her clit and the suggestion of pleasure wafted up through her chakras reminding her of him. Anything pleasurable brought her mind to him. Gunnar was the only one who could ease her when her body started to relapse into a CPTSD spiral. She squeezed eyes shut and prayed for any thoughts of him to take this all away. Any thought would do.

Her mind went racing as to why he hadn't contacted her and instead contacted Aileen. She thought he probably even talked with Jo instead of her and she just couldn't understand why. *How could he tell me he loves me then refuse to speak to me? Why has he not contacted me?*

She slowed her breathing and tried to calm her mind. A memory flowed in, and she allowed it. She remembered one time when Gunnar had placed his gun and wallet to the side on the desk at her old roomie's house. He'd turned to her, cradling her lower back with one hand and using the other up the front of her shirt to unclasp her bra. She'd let it fall to the floor and grabbed at his workout shirts, lifting them up and over his head. His beautifully sculpted chest and neck were exposed and Peg went in to nibble all around his ear and then down his neck and stomach. He'd lifted her face to his and kissed her, backing her up against the bed so he could remove her jeans. He'd taken his shoes off and pulled his pants down, stepping on them to get them off quicker. Peg had reached for his rigid dick, loving how engorged he was for her.

"You...are so wanted, baby..." she'd whispered into the quiet of the room, making him smile. She'd taken him fully into her mouth, leaving him gasping for breath. Peg had moved slowly up and down his shaft, feeling him pulse from the pleasure.

"Oh my...baby...ohhhhhh...*Peg*...." He'd brought his hand down, cradling her face. He'd absolutely loved the way she gave him head. He'd never had it the way Peg did it. She'd been so gentle but eager, as if she really cared about his pleasure and the build-up. Feeling her tongue and lips swirling and caressing him, all of him, he'd gasped. She'd taken each ball into her mouth, giving one just as much attention as the other. After a while, she'd got up and pointed to the area of the bed she'd wanted him on.

"Lie here?"

"Okay." He'd watched her as she made sure he was comfortable and then she'd put a drop of lube on her finger. Next, she'd opened his legs and climbed onto the bed in between them. Gunnar had moaned, not knowing what she was planning but knowing everything she did was pleasurable and tender.

She'd slid her mouth over him again and he'd sucked air in through his teeth, watching her slide her lips and mouth further, down to his base. He'd relaxed, leaning his head back against the pillow, and she'd inserted her lubed finger into his anal opening. Gunnar gasped louder, loving the feeling of her finger sliding warm and slow into him. The feel of her sucking his head and shaft, along with her slow rhythmic fingering, had been mind-blowing. He'd felt he was getting too close and had been about to explode. He'd reached out and gently grabbed her under her arms.

"Kiss me?"

Peg had followed his request and straddled him, kissing him deep while sinking half-way down on him slow.

"Oh wow...you are so wet baby...you're dripping...."

"I'm sorry."

"Please don't apologize..."

"Do you...?"

"Do I?"

She'd smiled, "Do you give consent?" She giggled knowing she was late in asking but loving their inside joke.

"Please?"

Peg had pushed onto him deeper, sliding his hard dick in and up inside her in one thrust. Gunnar had gasped again. Peg exhaled her pleasure. He'd filled and stretched her in a way that made her want to give him all of her. She thrust...and thrust and caressed...and thrust so slow, taking him into her, squeezing and then releasing him for another deep thrust.

Gunnar had grabbed at her ass, holding on, letting her take him, surrendering as she had requested. Peg had ridden him for what seemed like hours. She felt he so big and fierce inside her. He'd especially liked how she'd sunk so deep on him that he could feel her cervix suckling his head and her clit rubbing on his pubic bone. Peg knew how to fuck, she had been all about slow pleasure, not only his, but matching his with her own, and he'd felt that was beyond hot. She'd known what she'd wanted, and he'd thought she was the sexiest woman he'd ever met.

She'd lifted up and before he knew what was happening, she'd crouched down between his legs again to take him into her mouth! He'd only been able to take the extreme pleasure for a few seconds before he'd had to stop her.

"I'm going to cum if you keep this up." He'd got up and reached for the honey whiskey on the desk and uncapped it taking a huge swig.

Peg stood up to stretch her legs and watch him. She'd smiled and walked towards him, caressing his tight muscular ass. He'd put the bottle down and turned to push her to the bed. He bent her over and sunk deep into her from behind.

Peg moaned and braced herself, taking in all his desire and realizing he wanted to take over. He'd driven into her, whispering to her about how he couldn't believe how she'd taken him into her mouth and pleased him until he'd almost exploded, and then ridden him like no other woman had. Gunnar had grabbed on either side of her hips, supporting them both, and had driven in deeper, causing her to cry out and press her palms against the wall so she could push back and meet his every move.

"Oh my god, the way you push back makes me feel so wanted, Peg. You are amazing..."

Peg smiled, pushing again. "I like what you do to my body..."

"I'm going to cum, baby..."

Peg had picked up the pace to make him feel all of her as he came. With a few more deep thrusts, Gunnar gripped her hips and had gone silent while Peg pushed back on him over and over and over until she'd heard him inhale and felt him pulse and release. His cum spilled inside her while his hands loosened, and his legs began to relax. He'd caught his breath and she'd waited patiently.

Gunnar pulled out and flipped her over onto her back. He'd pressed his mouth into her and begun flicking his tongue along her clit until she'd curled up into him. Her arms flew back and she'd pushed against the wall feeling his glorious mouth on her.

His tongue felt amazing, and suddenly Peg felt her eruption come crashing down on her. She'd screamed his name into the room making an echo. He'd smiled, and moaned, loving how pleased she had been. It aroused him and he had been happy to feel himself hard again.

He'd lifted away and Peg's arms came in to cradle her breasts, her legs closing to squeeze every ounce of throbbing orgasm through her yoni. She'd turned to her side to recover, and he'd taken the opportunity to lie behind her and put his arms around her while pressing his cock between her thighs. She'd arched back, opening to receive him and he'd slid slick into her womb again, filling her as he'd grown hard again, making her gasp in her post-orgasmic sensitivity.

Peg's head flew back and he'd cradled it with his chest and took both her breasts in his palms, driving deeper and deeper into her. She'd moaned with pleasure, and he'd sunk his mouth deep into her neck, causing her to cry out in ecstasy! Goosebumps and shivers had run through her and she'd clenched around his dick harder.

Gunnar bit her gently then asked, "Would you ride me again?"

Peg nodded and he'd helped her to her feet. He laid down on the bed and instead of straddling him, she turned around and sunk down on him in reverse cowgirl.

Gunnar was very pleased, "Oh wow baby...I love when you do this..."

Peg had begun swaying and swirling her hips slowly and had built up to a faster pace. Gunnar loved to see her move and reached forward to open her tush and watch her move up and down on his shaft. He'd murmured how beautiful they were together and how hot she was. It aroused Peg to hear his gratification and she picked up the pace, moving and humping him rapidly.

Gunnar sucked air in through his teeth and began to clench at her hips. Peg felt him start to cum again and she went wild, making sure he surrendered. They both released and yelled into the tiny room, crashing over into pure bliss...*together.*

Peg heard a knock at Aileen's front door, and it startled her from her tantric meditations. She remembered the danger and suddenly her heart was racing! Her memories could sooth her for a little while, but the reality was that Dereck still wanted her... *dead.*

Josephine breezed into the living room with Aileen shuffling along behind her. She looked at Peg and her eyes softened. She couldn't believe the nightmare was on again. Peg had come so far in her healing just to be terrified again. Josephine knew Peg's type of PTSD must be off the charts since Aileen had told her about Dereck's murders.

"Hey there. How ya holding up?"

Peg sat up, looking groggy, her panties wet from dreaming of Gunnar.

"I'm happy to be here with you both instead of dead in my roommate's foyer." She huffed a laugh but was met with only pitying looks from both of them.

"He just needs to die, Peg. He's a waste of human life. I've seen so many like him in my previous work. They add no value to the human race."

Jo looked up at Aileen, "Wow Ai, I've never heard you say that before."

"I've about had it with Dereck Law. If he were here right now, I'd put a bullet between his eyes and do the world a favor."

Peg stared up at her, wondering if she'd found out more about him in the last hour.

"Jeez, down girl." Jo giggled and looked at Peg.

Aileen wasn't finished. "I'm serious, He's like the fucked up runt of the litter that the mother dog eats to save the rest of the pups. He should have been aborted."

Both Peg and Jo stared at her shocked at her words. Jo stepped back. "Ai, have you been hitting the whiskey? I mean I can't say I don't agree...it's just you usually text this shit. I've never heard you calmly say such beautifully horrible things."

Peg interjected. "Um, what's weird, Aileen is...well, Dereck used to say that puppy comment about martial art students in class he didn't like or who made him look bad...and oddly, his mother had once admitted she should have aborted him when she was in one of her trauma rages. You're blowing my mind here."

Aileen walked to her chaise and slumped down in it, exhaling. "I'm sorry. I guess I have no filter tonight. How ya doing Jo?"

Peg watched as Josephine sat down and she spoke to them before Jo could answer.

"Firstly, could we please discuss how both of you have talked with Gunnar...and I...*have not*? I mean, could you explain to me why? How is it he can so freely talk with you both but can't contact me or let me know if he's safe? What...did I do?"

Aileen's phone vibrated in her pocket.

Chapter 21

OVER

Peg opened the door to the laundry room and continued on to the door leading to Aileen's garage. She was grateful to be able to hide her truck in Aileen's overly large and unused garage which made her truck look smaller than it actually was. Making her way around to the passenger side, she opened the door but felt an odd chill down her spine. She squinted her eyes and hoped she wasn't coming down with anything. Soaking in a tub full of Epsom salt was probably what she needed. Sleeping at Aileen's was going to be tough enough, a hot bath would definitely help.

Reaching into her overnight bag she, rummaged around for a few items. The bag slid off the beautiful gun box underneath and her eyes fixed on it. Her heart began to ache again as visions of Gunnar ran through her mind. Half of her was pissed he'd talked to both Josephine and Aileen, the other half loved him more, for thinking of her safety. She tried to shove both feelings down and calm her racing heart wondering when, if ever, memories of him would cease to make her so emotional.

"There she is-" Dereck cocked the gun and pointed it right at her face.

Peg jumped and pushed her back against the door facing him.

"Careful there, Ms. Thang. No sudden movements."

"Fuck you."

The words seethed through her teeth; she hardly recognized her own voice. Her heart pounded almost painfully against the inside of her ribcage.

He smirked. "Ah, angry are we? How's that feel going down?"

Peg looked into his dead, black eyes. She knew he was the killer he'd proven. All the years of knowing him, defending him, raising a family with him-it all meant nothing. He was dead inside. He always had been and she knew it now. There weren't many people she hated but she knew she this man. She'd heard his mother in her ears saying she should have aborted him...and now she agreed. She could see he liked that she was backed against the door, trapped again, like she had been in her marriage with him. Suddenly, a calmness washed over her. She didn't care anymore. She didn't have Gunnar, she didn't have security anymore, she didn't have the drive to keep fighting anymore.

Peg looked him up and down and couldn't understand one horrible human had so much power to ruin lives. He was nothing in her eyes. Her shoulders dropped and she just accepted she was cornered, at his mercy, just as he'd wanted.

"What? No smart-ass remark? No answer from the beloved Pegasus Law?'

"No longer *Law*...soon to be O'Clery."

Dereck grimaced. "Uh, I'm pretty sure we're still married as I have not signed shit."

"I don't need your signature."

"So that's how it's goin' to be, huh? You found your happily-ever-after Peg? We were just nothing? Just space in time until you found your forever guy? And how long ago did you figure all this out? Bet you wanted him for years, huh?"

She lowered her voice. "Only every time I closed my eyes and had to try to get off on your baby dick."

Dereck pushed the gun at her flicking it closer to her face. She didn't even blink. Peg didn't care anymore. If she was going to die this way...by his hand...she was going to let him know the truth.

"You've got to be the stupidest bitch ever."

"Only for believing in us. All those years you kept so many secrets. That underage girl, my friend Kim, Dean, Lauren, her underage daughters, my mom, the karate students, the men, the single moms, the foster kids...you fucking R Kelly wannabe! A coward on the inside, thinking you could run a kingdom on the outside. You're a fucking joke, Dereck. A waste of human flesh. Your mother was righ-"

Dereck stepped forward abruptly and came down on her cheekbone with the butt of the gun. He stepped back to watch her recover, his lips quivering, rage coursing through him.

Peg lifted her head and stared at him. She knew she was getting to him and was happy that moments earlier, she had opened the gun box on her front seat. He might put a bullet in her again but, she was hopeful the Barretta Gunnar had gifted her would give her a chance to take him out too.

"So, now you've actually left a mark. All those years of almost hitting me, letting me trip into walls, bumping me with your hands in your pockets so you could maintain that you 'never hit women'...Well, today you became "that guy". A killer, a molester, a pedophile, and now a domestic violence abuser. Wow, you must be so proud of yourself Dereck. You are the full package. A complete piece-of-shit human with probably the tiniest package I've ever felt."

"You cunt!" Dereck lunged forward, grabbing at her shoulders, the gun still in one hand, and pulled her away from the truck door and throwing her to the garage floor. Peg rolled into it and out, standing up, and backing up away from him towards the garage door. She could hear footsteps outside the door. She spoke to cover it and hoped it was Josephine.

"Oh wow. Disrespectful and abusive. You're really turning me on Dereck." She was sure to raise her voice just enough to identify him.

He stepped fast towards her, the gun still in his right hand but no interest in it. He clearly intended to beat the shit out of her first.

Dereck lunged again. Peg torqued left then dodged right and step around him swiftly, striking as hard as she could on his ear, remembering his sensitive trigeminal nerve near his masseter muscle and temporal bones.

Dereck winced then cursed loudly. Peg felt satisfaction at successfully hindering him. She dashed towards the passenger seat and slid her hand under the overnight bag finding the cold steel of the gun. She was clumsy as her right hand was not her favored shooting hand, but he'd shot her before on her left side. She knew not to depend on that arm. Hearing him behind her and knowing he would come at her, Peg crouched down and aimed. Dereck had not been expecting her to point a gun at him; he'd underestimated her...*again*. He raised his gun up but she fell to the ground and aimed. He shot...she shot.

Then she shot two more times.

Darkness encircled her and all sound dissolved into to a high-pitched ringing...then quieted. It was over.

Gunnar lifted the garage door, breaking the opener springs. He didn't care. He saw her. He saw *him*. Lifeless. He holstered his gun and ran to her on the cold cement floor. He kicked Dereck's gun away from his hand and stood over her.

"Oh no. Peg!!"

He gazed down at her, the gun he'd given her still in her hand, blood splattered all over her beautiful skin. He knelt down, grabbing her, pulling her into him as he slumped down, cradling her to his chest. His heart raced as her limp body felt warm against his. He'd missed her so much.

"Baby, please. Peg? *Baby please*. It's me. I'm here. It's me, Peg. I'll never leave you again. I should have never...*Peg*!!!"

Chapter 22

ALWAYS BEEN YOU

Gunnar picked up his cell and smiled as he looked at it. Josephine and Aileen had come through for him and the moment he'd been waiting for was finally going to take place. He couldn't wait to see her face when he finally revealed his truth. If anyone deserved happiness, it was Peg. She gave so much, never asking much in return and he was going to spend the rest of his life making sure he returned happiness to her.

Turning to look back at his empty office, he lifted his hand to the light switch. He'd done well here, for over thirty years, but it was time to start the new life he wanted, with the person he'd dreamt of doing it with. When the lights went out, he closed the door, and walked away from all that he knew of being a cop. He'd served the people of Las Ramas well, but now he wanted to serve his woman well, if she'd have him.

Peg was still not sure she would show up. How Jo and Aileen had convinced her to go with them to Gunnar's retirement party was beyond her. She loved him, but she didn't want to see him say goodbye to all he knew of law enforcement and all the people he'd worked with. Seeing Gunnar in any sort of pain tore at her deeply.

She knew she'd never loved this way before and if it were anyone else, she'd have flat out said no. Truth be told, he was the most important person in her life. He'd made it clear, by finding her on that garage floor after killing Dereck, that he was her person. He always had been. She'd just waited a lifetime for a love like theirs.

She stepped into a little black dress and made sure to strap on Gunnar's favorite black heels-which she'd been able to put to use again as their love affair picked up right where it left off-albeit reaching commitment status from the first night. He'd divorced, she was widowed, and without missing a beat, the mind-blowing sex had gotten even steamier. He'd been in her bed every night. Being apart wasn't even a thought anymore. Peg had gladly put the past in the past and looked forward to each new day.

There were no parking spots outside of the lodge and cars were lined up down the street. She wasn't surprised since Gunnar was the department's most senior officer and extremely popular. She felt a tightness in her stomach and wanted to turn around and go home for fear of everyone staring at her as the woman whose ex had tried to kill her, and who'd had to kill him in self-defense. Then there was the little fact that she was the girlfriend of Las Ramas' most decorated officer. She hated that she still cared about the gossip, but it was partly because she didn't want to bring drama to Gunnar's life.

He'd told her over and over again how honored he was that she accepted him back into her life after he'd left. It had been hard for her to hear that Dereck had been with Gunnar's ex and lied about so much. Gunnar and her had already separated but Dereck had sealed the deal for divorce. He'd even slept with Gunnar's ex at her office.

Peg had apologized to Gunnar when he'd told her. She'd felt awful when she'd seen the pain in Gunnar's eyes as he'd explained how Dereck had ruined his marriage years ago. He was the guy his wife had cheated on him with at work, but no one had known it. He'd admitted to Peg that what Dereck had done wrecked his family but had also brought him to her, for which he was grateful. He'd told her there was nothing better than being able to love her.

Peg smiled at the memory of his words as she finally found a space to park far down the road from the building. As she hopped down out of the truck, Jo and Aileen pulled up.

"*There* you are, you sexy beast. Get your ass in here. I'm taking you in those heels, along with gimpy here, to the front door. I'll have one of those young officers valet us." Jo shouted through the open window.

Peg bent in and smiled admiring how they'd dressed up for the retirement party. Aileen looked Peg up and down as well, wavering her eyebrows.

"Jo, there ain't no valet parking, you twit." Aileen murmured.

Peg laughed and jumped into the backseat of Jo's Range Rover.

"Well, we're creating valet service tonight. I know I can get an officer to park this and walk back with my keys. I'll just tell him I've got Gunnar O'Clery's hot ass girlfriend with me."

"Not so sure that would-"

"Oh, stop it. That man loves the shit out of you and the whole town knows it."

Peg made eye contact with Jo in her rearview. "No they don't Jo.'

"Well, they should."

Aileen reached over, smacking Jo's shoulder lightly and giving her a look. "Would ya leave her alone, Jo. She's had more attention in this town than she needs. Let the child enjoy the evening."

"Oh, we're all going to enjoy this evening, especially Gunnar. Have you seen her fucking tan-ass legs in that dress and those heels?"

Peg laughed, "You're too kind."

"No, she's telling the truth, Peg. I saw you get out of your truck. You look amazing honey."

"Thank you."

"You know he's going to want to fuck you as soon as he sees you, right?" Jo was being spicy.

Peg smiled. "I'd much prefer that to having to watch three-hundred people whisper and judge me. When he fucks me, I feel like myself, at least."

Aileen turned to look at her. "Don't worry about the haters, baby girl. They're only hatin' because they see something they wish they were."

"Oh, yes. Everyone wants to be a woman who can shoot her ex in the eye, the chest, and crotch...killing him."

"Everyone thinks you're a hero, Peg. He killed an orderly, an elderly couple who stopped to help him, your neighbor, his son, and their fucking dog! You thwarted a psycho serial killer, woman. Who cares if you were married to him for twenty-two years."

Peg huffed. "I was married to a pedophile."

"All the more reason to put him down. You did a good thing, Peg. The's what heroes do. They defend themselves along with saving others. Who knows how many more he would have killed if he hadn't been shot...and with your fucking right hand too. You put three in him with your non-dominant shooting hand!"

Peg sat back against the seat, feeling nervous but grateful for what Aileen had said. The last year had been a special kind of hell but one she'd do all over again if it meant getting to love Gunnar.

Gunnar moved the microphone again so it was closer to his mouth. He hated speeches but had no choice as this was his last goodbye to all who knew him in law enforcement. His colleagues, his children, his peers, even college friends were all staring up at him on the stage. He had them laughing, even had some crying, and he was so honored that so many had come. It was almost time to eat but there was just one more thing he wanted to do and as he saw Peg come through the door at the back of the FOP lodge, he knew almost all his wishes were coming true.

Peg looked stunning in her classy little black dress with his favorite heels on. He could tell she was a bit nervous. He knew he'd change that, but she'd have to be brave for a bit, for him. He stopped mid-sentence, and everyone turned to look back at who he was smiling at. The room grew quiet.

Gunnar addressed her, causing her to stop in her tracks. "Pegasus Law, would you come up here for a moment, please?"

Peg tried to shake her head but both Jo and Aileen took her hands and started to walk with her.

Jo whispered. "We got you girl. Remember, this town ain't shit without you and him."

"Yeah, what she said." Aileen whispered. Peg realized if Aileen could get out in public, she could do it too.

Peg made it to the stairs. They both let her go and nudged her towards Gunnar's waiting hand. He guided her up the steps and kissed her deeply in front of everyone. She felt relaxation wash over her in his arms, even though the was their first time being seen in public together. He always calmed her.

"I love you, darling. Come stand over here with me."

Peg looked out over the crowd and could see what seemed like a million curious eyes staring back at her. Gunnar had her stand in front of him and he brought the microphone to his mouth.

"Baby? I know you don't much appreciate me bringing you up here, what with all you've been through this year. I just want these folks to know what kind of gal I have."

He looked out over the crowd and continued, "Yes, this is my gal, my best friend, my partner, and the best soul I've ever met. "

Gunnar turned back towards Peg, who had tears beginning in the corners of her eyes.

"Peg...it's you baby. It's always been you. I've loved you for years, I just didn't know it. You are my other half, the best part of me. I don't ever want a day to go by without seeing your sweet face near me on my pillow. This...none of this works for me without you. And I know this retirement might require some adjustment, as I learn to be something other than an officer. I've got plans to travel the world and I know you want to write books. I guess...what I want to ask is would you maybe wanna do that together as husband and...*wife?*"

Peg brought her hand up to her mouth in disbelief. She couldn't believe this was happening. All she'd ever wanted, all her dreams, the love she'd thought she had to bury deep down...it was all there, standing in front of her, in him.

Gunnar knelt down and opened a tiny black box, to her revealing the biggest engagement ring she'd ever seen up close. "Pegasus Aine Law, would you do me the honor of becoming Pegasus Aine O'Clery...and making me the happiest man alive?"

Peg's knees buckled and she knelt down in front of him taking his face in her hands and kissing him deeply. Her body melded to his as he wrapped his strong arms around her, allowing the rest of the world to fall away.

Allowing time to pause...and slow...as the ellipses would...

their ellipses...

DEZI GOLDEN is an American Author from Las Cruces, New Mexico. This is her ninth novel. Find Dezi online or write to her at dezigolden@gmail.com. Autographed copies are available.

The author would like to acknowledge:

That the characters, plot, places, timing, and intimacy in this novel are fictitious. It is not to offend anyone's personal preferences, gender, culture, or history.

Gratitude to those who shared their experiences and time while research for the story's characters, scenarios, plot, and careers was being developed.

Thank you for purchasing this book published by Author, Dezi Golden.

To receive an autographed copy for your collection. Contact the author at dezigolden.com or dezigolden@gmail.com.

www.ingramcontent.com/pod-product-compliance
Lightning Source LLC
Chambersburg PA
CBHW031427200626
46814CB00016B/2707